Never Say Never

By Danielle Steel

NEVER SAY NEVER • TRIAL BY FIRE • TRIANGLE • JOY • RESURRECTION
ONLY THE BRAVE • NEVER TOO LATE • UPSIDE DOWN • THE BALL AT VERSAILLES
SECOND ACT • HAPPINESS • PALAZZO • THE WEDDING PLANNER
WORTHY OPPONENTS • WITHOUT A TRACE • THE WHITTIERS • THE HIGH NOTES
THE CHALLENGE • SUSPECTS • BEAUTIFUL • HIGH STAKES • INVISIBLE
FLYING ANGELS • THE BUTLER • COMPLICATIONS • NINE LIVES • FINDING ASHLEY
THE AFFAIR • NEIGHBORS • ALL THAT GLITTERS • ROYAL • DADDY'S GIRLS
THE WEDDING DRESS • THE NUMBERS GAME • MORAL COMPASS • SPY • CHILD'S PLAY
THE DARK SIDE • LOST AND FOUND • BLESSING IN DISGUISE • SILENT NIGHT
TURNING POINT • BEAUCHAMP HALL • IN HIS FATHER'S FOOTSTEPS • THE GOOD FIGHT
THE CAST • ACCIDENTAL HEROES • FALL FROM GRACE • PAST PERFECT • FAIRYTALE
THE RIGHT TIME • THE DUCHESS • AGAINST ALL ODDS • DANGEROUS GAMES
THE MISTRESS • THE AWARD • RUSHING WATERS • MAGIC • THE APARTMENT
PROPERTY OF A NOBLEWOMAN • BLUE • PRECIOUS GIFTS • UNDERCOVER • COUNTRY
PRODIGAL SON • PEGASUS • A PERFECT LIFE • POWER PLAY • WINNERS • FIRST SIGHT
UNTIL THE END OF TIME • THE SINS OF THE MOTHER • FRIENDS FOREVER • BETRAYAL
HOTEL VENDÔME • HAPPY BIRTHDAY • 44 CHARLES STREET • LEGACY • FAMILY TIES
BIG GIRL • SOUTHERN LIGHTS • MATTERS OF THE HEART • ONE DAY AT A TIME
A GOOD WOMAN • ROGUE • HONOR THYSELF • AMAZING GRACE • BUNGALOW 2
SISTERS • H.R.H. • COMING OUT • THE HOUSE • TOXIC BACHELORS • MIRACLE
IMPOSSIBLE • ECHOES • SECOND CHANCE • RANSOM • SAFE HARBOUR
JOHNNY ANGEL • DATING GAME • ANSWERED PRAYERS • SUNSET IN ST. TROPEZ
THE COTTAGE • THE KISS • LEAP OF FAITH • LONE EAGLE • JOURNEY
THE HOUSE ON HOPE STREET • THE WEDDING • IRRESISTIBLE FORCES
GRANNY DAN • BITTERSWEET • MIRROR IMAGE • THE KLONE AND I
THE LONG ROAD HOME • THE GHOST • SPECIAL DELIVERY • THE RANCH
SILENT HONOR • MALICE • FIVE DAYS IN PARIS • LIGHTNING • WINGS • THE GIFT
ACCIDENT • VANISHED • MIXED BLESSINGS • JEWELS • NO GREATER LOVE • HEARTBEAT
MESSAGE FROM NAM • DADDY • STAR • ZOYA • KALEIDOSCOPE • FINE THINGS
WANDERLUST • SECRETS • FAMILY ALBUM • FULL CIRCLE • CHANGES
THURSTON HOUSE • CROSSINGS • ONCE IN A LIFETIME • A PERFECT STRANGER
REMEMBRANCE • PALOMINO • LOVE: *POEMS* • THE RING • LOVING
TO LOVE AGAIN • SUMMER'S END • SEASON OF PASSION • THE PROMISE
NOW AND FOREVER • PASSION'S PROMISE • GOING HOME

Nonfiction

EXPECT A MIRACLE: *Quotations to Live and Love By*
PURE JOY: *The Dogs We Love*
A GIFT OF HOPE: *Helping the Homeless*
HIS BRIGHT LIGHT: *The Story of Nick Traina*

For Children

PRETTY MINNIE IN PARIS
PRETTY MINNIE IN HOLLYWOOD

DANIELLE STEEL

Never Say Never

A Novel

Delacorte Press | New York

Published in the United States by Delacorte Press, an imprint of Random House, a division of Penguin Random House LLC, New York.

Delacorte Press is a registered trademark and the DP colophon is a trademark of Penguin Random House LLC.

Hardback ISBN 978-0-593-49864-4
Ebook ISBN 978-0-593-49865-1

Printed in the United States of America on acid-free paper

randomhousebooks.com

2 4 6 8 9 7 5 3 1

First Edition

To my beloved children,
Beatrix, Trevor, Todd,
Nick, Samantha, Victoria,
Vanessa, Maxx, and Zara,

May you find the right people
to love and love you.
May you be brave, safe, and loved.
May you find joy
and be blessed always.

With all my heart and love,
     Mom / D. S.

Never Say Never

Chapter 1

Oona Kelly Webster put the finishing touches on the Thanksgiving table with a critical eye, and made sure it looked as perfect as she wanted it, and her family expected it to be. Everything in Oona's life was orderly, and impeccably planned well in advance. She didn't like surprises, and tried to anticipate problems so that they would never happen. She'd had an impressive career in publishing at Hargrove Publishers, a small but highly respected house that existed under the umbrella of a larger publishing conglomerate. She had worked at the same company since she'd graduated from Princeton, and had taken classes from some of the greatest contemporary writers of our time.

From junior editor, over time she had risen to being the head of the small but most lofty literary imprint, publishing exceptionally fine authors. The house was prestigious, although its revenues did not compare to those that published commercial fiction. And as the publisher of her own imprint, Oona Kelly was a greatly respected, distinguished person in the literary world. She was very proud of the talented authors she had discovered, even if their sales figures were not as high as the blockbuster bestsellers of commercial fiction. Their work was for an elite readership who preferred obscure literary work, of a more intellectual nature.

Now almost forty-seven, Oona had discovered and published many very fine writers, several of whom were famous. She nurtured and encouraged her authors with great care. Unlike the world of bestselling commercial fiction, hers was not a dog-eat-dog existence. It was one of dignity, finesse, and great literary minds. As head of the house, she had a protected and very secure situation, with considerable prestige. She didn't abuse the power she had, but she enjoyed her position and all that it entailed.

In spite of the highbrow literary nature of the books she published, Oona looked a decade younger than her age, and the older authors whom she published were surprised and delighted to meet a pretty young woman with big green eyes, a youthful face, and a warm smile, who understood and appreciated their work, and had an excellent education and twenty-five years of experience. She was dedicated to the imprint she represented and to its authors, and defended their interests fiercely. She got them the best advances she could, given their somewhat limited sales. The owners of the publishing house were a brilliant, astute family who had owned it for three generations and grown their overall publishing, including nonfiction, some carefully selected fiction, and academic textbooks that were lucrative, into a massive multibillion-dollar business. They valued Oona's contributions, and the high-end relatively small imprint she ran. It wasn't a big moneymaker but it gave them a great deal of prestige in the publishing world. And keeping it small gave Oona the opportunity to run it impeccably, with full control of every detail, which was how she ran her personal life and home as well.

She had married Charles Webster six months after graduating from Princeton, and she was already working at Hargrove Publishing then. Charles was twelve years older, and thirty-four at the time. He was already a successful account executive in advertising and enjoyed it thoroughly. They had met at a party in New York, where they both lived, and had grown up, and it was a whirlwind romance, which turned into a solid marriage, with their two children, Meghan and Will, who were twenty-two and twenty-four now. Will was born on their first anniversary and Oona went back to work six weeks later because she loved her job. Oona and Charles both had big careers, busy lives, and too little time together, but they tried to have dinner together once a week. The kids were out of the house now.

Oona and Charles were about to celebrate their twenty-fifth anniversary in December, and had decided to put off a big party until the spring. Instead they had rented a very handsome house in France, an hour outside Paris, near Milly-la-Forêt in the department of Essonne. She and Charles were going to spend a month there from mid-February to mid-March. They were hoping that their children, Meghan and Will, would join them for a week, and the rest of the time they were going to enjoy three weeks alone in France. It was something they had said they had wanted to do for years, so Oona had organized it. The house looked beautiful and had a housekeeper who came on weekdays. The home and property seemed grander than what they needed, but they had decided to spoil themselves. It was owned by a Hong Kong Chinese family that rented the home out for weddings, and occasionally to foreigners looking for a comfortable, luxurious vacation experience in a lovely location.

Charles and Oona had both worked during their entire marriage, cared equally about their family and their careers, and had reached considerable status in their respective professional communities at a young age. Charles had switched to a more dynamic ad agency a decade earlier, and was the number two person at Hills, Rockwell, and Klein advertising. He'd been in line for the number one position for the past five years but had been passed over. Now he had to wait for another round, until the current CEO retired, which didn't appear to be imminent, but Charles loved his job and didn't mind the wait for the top position. He liked working there in the meantime. It fed his ego and his mind. He had status, respect, great perks, and fewer headaches than he would have had as CEO.

Their daughter, Meghan, was due to return to New York by the end of the year. She had graduated from George Washington University in Washington, D.C., in June, with a major in Global Philanthropy, and she was currently finishing an internship sponsored by the Carter Foundation, which had several programs in Africa that interested her. And she was looking for a long-term job, hopefully abroad for a few years.

Will had gone to UC Berkeley, graduated three years before, had stayed in San Francisco, and worked for Google, which he loved.

He thrived on the California life—the weather, the athletics, the outdoors. He had no desire to move back to New York.

Their father, Charles, was fifty-nine, and was determined to become CEO of HRK before he retired. It was his one major goal. The status it would bring with it was important to him, which he admitted sheepishly to Oona at times, although his role as second in line to the throne was not an unpleasant one, and he had sufficient power to keep him happy in the meantime. But he wanted to achieve the status of CEO before he retired.

Both their children were on well-thought-out career paths, having been taught since early on to do so, although Oona was less pleased with Meghan's determination to spend the next several years in underdeveloped countries, improving the lot of suffering people. She didn't like the idea of Meghan going someplace dangerous, which was part of what appealed to Meghan. She couldn't see herself wasting her time in some insignificant underpaid glamour job, like many of her friends working for the assistant beauty editors of major magazines. She wanted to make a difference in the world, face-to-face and hand to hand, on the ground, which Charles heartily approved of. Oona was concerned about the dangers of being exposed to tribal wars, health risks, and the threats to any beautiful woman as young as she was. But Meghan was strong-willed and almost sure to do what she wanted in the end, and Oona was bracing herself for it, once Meghan started looking for jobs in earnest at various foundations in New York that had projects and staff abroad.

Meghan and Will were both coming home for Thanksgiving, as

they always did, and their parents were going to tell them then about the house they had rented in France. Oona and Charles were both excited about it, and Oona, reading up on the local history, had already discovered that the house had an interesting history of its own. It had been built by Louis XVI, the last French king before the Revolution, for his favorite mistress, and it was named after her, "La Belle Florence." It had numerous secret passages, and originally had a tunnel joining it to a nearby château, where the king had spent a great deal of his time, when that mistress was his favorite. She had died young, in mysterious circumstances, and he was said to be heartbroken at the time. The château where he had stayed had burned during the French Revolution and was gone, but the home of the king's mistress was still standing, and had been lovingly restored and maintained by its various owners during the centuries since. It seemed like a romantic spot to spend their anniversary, and Charles was amused by Oona's fascination with it.

Their own relationship wasn't romantic, or demonstrative, and never had been, but it was warm, comfortable, predictable, and solid. With two busy professional lives, their paths often ran parallel rather than intersecting as often as they wished. But they tried to make up for it with family vacations in the summer, and dinner dates once a week, when their schedules allowed. The intention was to catch up on what was happening in their respective lives. Sometimes they didn't have a chance to talk at length for days. There were times when Oona felt they didn't communicate enough, but it was hard to stay on top of everything with business lives as demanding as theirs. They saw more of each other when the children were home, but that didn't happen often now, with their children living in other cities, with busy lives of their own. Their careers mattered to all four of them. And success was something they were expected to achieve, even in philanthropy. Oona and Charles had taught their children the value of work and set a strong example for it. Neither of the children was lazy, both had been good students, and they had gotten good grades. Oona considered both their marriage and their family a success, which mattered to her even more than it did to Charles, who was a little less demanding of the children than his wife. Oona wanted her children to be happy, but she wanted them to work hard too.

Oona's father had been a hard-driving venture capitalist who had flown his own plane on the weekends and had been killed in a crash during a winter storm when she was ten. Her mother had never recovered, had withdrawn from the world, and died at an early age of cancer when Oona was in college. Her mother was an intelligent, capable woman, but had never had a job. She was a talented artist, but never showed her work, and Oona had often wished that her mother would do something to use her talents in some way. Instead she had faded away like a ghost once her husband died, which made Oona even more determined to have a career, and never give up her job or her dreams that made her life worthwhile, gave her a feeling of self-worth, and grounded her, and she never had.

Charles had two brothers he wasn't close to, and all three boys were highly competitive with each other. In his family, they were expected to be outstanding athletes and have big careers, and were always pitted against each other by their domineering father. He was a merchant banker. The competition their parents fostered among them had driven the brothers apart at an early age. They had little in common except a desire to excel. Charles was the least aggressive of the three, and always had been. One of his brothers was in investments, a star on Wall Street, and the other was in the oil business, and had made a fortune of his own. Their wives were equally ambitious, embedded in various charities, serving on a broad variety of boards, and socially competitive. Oona didn't enjoy her sisters-in-law the rare times she saw them, and their children were as driven as they were. Although Charles's parents were moderately wealthy, enough to live well and educate their sons at the best schools, money was the driving force in the family, and Charles had always been more sensitive and humane than they were, which was why Oona loved him.

Both his brothers had told him to quit when he was passed over as CEO. Charles preferred to wait it out until the next round, which seemed reasonable to Oona too. He was a good father to their children and had been a good husband to her. Their relationship had never been passionate—in some ways at times they seemed more like friends than lovers—but they had been faithful to each other and were respectful partners. It seemed like enough to her. He never interfered in her career, or with the choices she made. He consulted her about the big decisions he made and respected her very sensible opinions.

As Oona looked the table over for the last time, she was satisfied with her family and marriage, and there was nothing she would have changed. One of the things she liked about their life was that it was predictable and stayed the same—there were no surprises or fast moves, no sudden shifts of direction. She knew what to expect, and what would happen when, which made her feel secure.

The children had come home the night before and were having breakfast together when she went back to the kitchen, to check on the progress of the turkey. She cooked the Thanksgiving meal herself every year, which satisfied her need for domesticity. Now that the children were gone, they had no set time for dinner, and no one to prepare it. She and Charles fended for themselves when they came home at night, and only made a point of having dinner together once a week. The rest of the time, Charles usually came home late, either after meetings or dinner with clients. Oona frequently had dinner with one of her authors or came home with a manuscript to read and comment on. On the weekends, she did errands or occasionally had lunch with a friend, and Charles played golf with clients or business associates. They had a weekend house in East Hampton, which they went to in the summer, but rarely on winter weekends. They used it less and less now that the children lived in other cities. Charles and Oona both found the house isolating and depressing in the winter months.

"What are you two up to?" Oona asked Meghan and Will, sitting at the kitchen table. She basted the turkey and joined them.

"Just talking," Will said vaguely. He was a handsome, dark-haired boy like his father, tall and well built, although Charles's hair was streaked with gray now, which made him look a lot older. Meghan's hair was a dark auburn, unlike her mother's brighter red, and she had brown eyes, while Oona's were green. The freckles that had been the bane of Oona's existence as a child had faded with age. Oona was a true redhead, with the lively personality to go with it. Meghan was more reserved, although she spoke her mind when she wanted to. Will was generally uncommunicative when his parents were around. He never talked about his personal life except when forced to, often by his more extroverted sister.

"Can I tell?" Meghan mouthed at him. He hesitated and then shrugged and nodded yes, and hoped he wouldn't regret it. "Will has a new girlfriend," she informed her mother, and Oona looked immediately interested.

"What happened to the Chinese girl from Singapore?" Oona asked him. She came from an important family and had gone to Stanford.

"She went home, to work for her father," he said in a dry tone. He didn't seem upset about it.

"This one is from Salt Lake City, she's twenty-seven years old, and Will works for her. She's his Division Manager," Meghan reported, and Oona nodded and turned to her son.

"Is that awkward, dating your boss?"

"It could be. We haven't told anyone at work. If it goes on, we'll have to tell them, and they'll transfer one of us to another section. I don't mind." He had always been mature for his age, and it didn't surprise Oona that the woman he was seeing was older than he was. Will was good-natured and easygoing, Meghan was more forceful about the subjects she cared about, and always the champion of the underdog and the underprivileged. Her internships so far had suited her, working for foundations involved with the indigent around the world.

"That's too bad if you have to be the one to transfer," his mother said, and he didn't comment. Oona wanted to ask him if she was worth his having to transfer but she didn't dare. He was old enough to make his own decisions about his job, she thought, and his romances.

They each spent the Thanksgiving day relaxing and doing whatever they wanted. Meghan and Will hung out together and went for a walk. They hadn't seen each other since a week at the house in the Hamptons in August, and they wanted to catch up.

At six o'clock they met in the living room of their spacious apartment on the Upper East Side, where they had grown up. They each had a glass of wine, talking animatedly, in good spirits. Charles had been out all day playing golf with friends. They sat down to dinner at seven and enjoyed the meal Oona had been cooking all afternoon. It was delicious, as it always was. Oona had perfected the meal for years and eliminated the mistakes. She included everyone's favorites, and over dessert they talked about the house they'd rented in France. Will promised to arrange for vacation time, and Meghan said she would tell anyone who interviewed her for a job that she needed the week off for a family event. Charles was quiet when they talked about it, letting Oona do the planning she was so good at, and she told them about the history of the house, which interested her more than the others. It was a lovely Thanksgiving. And the kids were excited about the week in France for their parents' anniversary.

The rest of the weekend went quickly, and on Sunday Meghan went back to Washington, D.C., and Will flew back to San Francisco. They would be home again for Christmas, and Meghan would be moving back from Washington then, unless she found a long-term job before that.

The house was quiet after they left. Oona made a light supper of leftovers, and she and Charles sat at the kitchen table. Charles was lost in thought, and eating slowly, picking at his food, and then he looked at Oona. He didn't know where to start, but he knew he had to tell her.

"I didn't want to spoil your plans in France with the kids, and I know you want them to come," he started.

"Don't you?" She looked surprised. "We said we'd spend a week with them, and three weeks on our own. That ought to be enough for us." She smiled at him, but she could see that he looked troubled. He looked pale as he gazed at her.

"I can't come," he said quietly.

"You can't? Why not? Something with a client?" She knew it had to be important for him to back out of their plans. "Do you want me to try to change the dates for the house?" He shook his head. Her world was about to crash around her and she didn't know it. He looked at her again.

"I'm not going with you, Oona. I'm really sorry. I don't even know where to start. I need a change. A big change. It's been a hard decision. I'm going to take a sabbatical."

"For a year?" She looked shocked. He had never mentioned it before, nor consulted her about the decision. He presented it as a fait accompli, which wasn't like him.

"Maybe. I'm going to start with six months."

"And do what? Why didn't you tell me?"

"It's complicated." And then something dawned on Oona that had never occurred to her before.

"Is there someone else?" she asked in a choked voice, expecting him to say no. And instead he nodded. There were tears in his eyes. He knew this was going to be hard, but he hadn't realized how hard until he was telling her.

"It's been going on for a year, it's been driving me insane. I can't do this anymore, to you or myself. I need some time to figure out who I am, and what I want."

"You're my husband and our children's father. What is there to figure out? Who is she? It's been going on for a year? Is it someone at work?" If he had shot her, she couldn't have looked more shocked.

"It is someone at work," he said guiltily. "I never expected this to happen. I haven't played around before. It just happened, and it grew to proportions I never even imagined."

"Enough to throw our marriage away? Is she very young?" Her heart was pounding as she asked him.

"Thirty-four. It's been hard because we work together every day. I'm sorry, Oona, I know this is a mess. But I can't lie to you and sit in a house in France with you for a month." She realized as she listened to him that he had been out every night for months. It wasn't unusual in his business, and she hadn't paid attention to the increase in nights he was out. She trusted him. And whoever she was, she was thirteen years younger than Oona, and twenty-five years younger than Charles. It was a lot. Oona could easily imagine some sexy woman who had bewitched him. Charles had never seemed interested in other women before. Something had changed.

"Who is she?" Not that it mattered if he was in love with her.

"That's part of the problem," he said, exhaling slowly. "Something like this happened in college. It only happened once. I never told you, and it never happened again. I thought I was just crazy, young and drunk. Apparently not. It's not a woman, Oona. It's a man. I need to go away and figure this out, and what I want. I understand whatever you need to do about it. I have no right to ask for your indulgence on this. But I have to figure out the life I want to live. I can't lead a double life the way I have for the past year." Oona sat at the kitchen table, staring at him, trying to absorb what he had said. She tried to remember the last time they had made love and she couldn't. A month? Two? Three? Why hadn't she ever suspected it, and why hadn't he told her? "I thought it was just some passing insanity, but he's a good person. This isn't his fault. It's mine. I thought it was just physical at first, but it isn't. I love him. Not the way I love you. We don't have history, but I love him. It's a completely different relationship, but it has value too. There's no way to be fair to everyone. The whole situation isn't fair. Maybe I always had this in me, and I didn't want to face it. You and I have been like friends and roommates for twenty-five years. The physical side never seemed that important to either of us. We were busy with our kids and our careers. I don't know what to say, Oona. I'm sorry, I'm so sorry."

"And you're leaving your job for him?" She was as pale as Charles by then, as he nodded. "That's a big step." She tried to sound calmer than she felt. She wanted to cry but was fighting not to.

"My brothers were right. I should have left when I got passed over for CEO. This is just a delaying tactic, a way to figure out my life and the job. He came from our office in Buenos Aires, and he has to go back. His visa expires in January. He could only work here for a year. I'm going to go with him when he goes back. I thought that would be better for you too. I won't be making a spectacle of myself here and embarrassing you. I want to do this as cleanly and decently as I can while I figure it out."

"What are you going to tell the kids?" she said, dabbing at her eyes with a napkin on the table, as the tears snuck out.

"The truth. It is what it is. They can come and see me if they want, if they're willing. I'm not going to force them to do anything." He didn't have to deal with his parents, which was a mercy, since both of them had been very old and had died in the last two years. But his brothers would have a lot to say about his discovering he was gay at nearly sixty.

"So you're taking a time-out from marriage, fatherhood, and your job," she said grimly. "A clean sweep, as it were. And what am I supposed to do? Wait, while you figure out if it's him or me? That's a little rough." She was part angry, part panicked, and part devastated.

"You have to do what you want, and what's right for you," Charles said. "I'll continue paying for your expenses, but I have no right to ask you to wait. If you want a divorce, you can have it. If you'd rather just be separated, I'm okay with that too. You have a right to see other people if you want," he said. He was in no position to object to that and didn't want to. She needed to be free too. But dating someone else was the last thing on her mind as she listened to him. Or even their expenses. Their marriage, as they knew it, had just ended. She felt like a bomb had hit her.

"Never. I'm not going to date anyone in these circumstances," she said firmly. "Until half an hour ago, I thought we were married. You're my husband, for better or worse. I think this qualifies

17

as the latter. I never wanted to get divorced or be divorced. I thought people who love each other can always work it out, but this is pretty steep."

"Roberto feels terrible about it too. He didn't want to break up our marriage."

"But he did," she said, bleakly, trying to adjust to everything Charles had told her.

"No, I am, because it's the only fair thing to do. I don't want to sneak around the way I have been for the last year, or lie to you, or celebrate an anniversary that I'm not honoring." It was honest of him, but she still felt awful.

"I suppose it's decent of you," she said, wiping a tear off her cheek. Trying to comfort her would have been hypocritical of him. He wanted to be with Roberto now, not with Oona. "When are you leaving?" she asked him.

"I'm going to move out tonight. I don't think I should stay here anymore now that you know. I'll stay here over Christmas when the kids are home, if you want me to. I want to tell them then. And we leave for Buenos Aires on January second." That was six weeks away. "You'll know where to reach me. I'm not disappearing off the face of the earth," he tried to reassure her.

"Just out of my life. Didn't you ever suspect this before?"

"Not since college, and even then I thought it was some kind of one-time slip. Maybe I never wanted to face it before. But I had to once I met Roberto, and knew I loved him." Hearing him say it so directly made her stomach turn over.

"Twenty-five years is a long time to lie to yourself, and to me," she said, and he nodded. He didn't disagree with her. But it made sense to him now. Once he met Roberto he realized he hadn't been in love with Oona or even attracted to her in years. There was nothing effeminate about him, but he realized now that he was powerfully attracted to a man, not a woman. It was something he had never faced, until he was fifty-nine years old, hard as that was to believe. It had taken Roberto, a beautiful Argentine blond, blue-eyed man, of English origin on his father's side, like many Argentinians.

"How do you think the kids will react?" he asked her, with worried eyes.

"It'll be a shock, not just that you're in love with a man, but that you're leaving your job and moving to another country for six months or a year, or forever." Her eyes searched his, but there were no clear answers now, except that he was leaving her, and whatever happened now, their marriage was over. There was no coming back from this.

"Do you want a divorce?" he asked her.

"I guess it will come to that in the end, whatever happens. I don't want to give you an answer now. I need time to think too." Oona stood up. There was nothing more to say. She went to her study, to avoid him. He went to his dressing room to pack a few things. He had already moved some of his clothes to Roberto's apartment, without her knowing. He felt like a monster, having told her, but there was no way to avoid it anymore. She had taken it even more graciously than he had hoped. Somehow, it made it all feel worse. He was turning sixty, and he was leaving his job, his wife, his home, his country, and his kids, he was in love with a man, and changing his life completely in every way. It was terrifying and yet he knew it was what he wanted, what he felt he had to do.

Oona knew it happened to others, but never in a million years had she thought this would ever happen to her.

Chapter 2

The weeks between Thanksgiving and Christmas passed like a film in fast-forward for Oona. She kept wishing that she could stop the film to catch her breath. She knew that Charles was still in the city, and going to work at HRK, while living with Roberto. She kept having to remind herself that he was leaving her, already had, leaving his job at the end of the year on sabbatical, and leaving the country in five weeks. He never called her to see how she was. He had walked out of her life and into Roberto's. She saw that he put the same amount he always did in her household account, he even added a little extra, but in every other way, he had removed himself. It was almost as if he had died, and Oona was mourning the loss of their marriage.

Since the children knew nothing about it yet, she had to remind herself not to let anything slip when she spoke to them. Will was busy with his job at Google and his girlfriend, and less aware of nuances when speaking to his mother, which he didn't do often.

He called every week or two, and otherwise sent her texts. Meghan called more often and was more likely to hear something in her mother's voice. Oona had to make sure she sounded "up" when she spoke to her and didn't give any sign of how devastated she felt.

Oona felt as though the bottom had dropped out of her world. She kept asking herself if it was her fault. Had she failed as a wife? If she had tried harder, been less involved with her job, or been more aggressive sexually, would he still have fallen for Roberto? Or was she fighting something in his DNA that would have surfaced sooner or later? You didn't just change sexual orientation because your wife was busy at work, or didn't feel sexy after a long day at the office or taking care of the kids when they were still at home. There had been plenty of occasions, particularly on weekends, when she would have been willing and had tried to initiate sex with him, but he wasn't in the mood or was stressed over client presentations that hadn't gone well.

She was willing to admit that she hadn't been the perfect wife, and their bond had never been one of passion, but it still didn't explain Roberto and the fact that Charles admitted that he was in love with him. He seemed as startled by it as Oona was, but he was willing to leave an entire world for him and start a whole new life.

In some ways it was easier that he would be exploring the relationship a continent away. She didn't have to worry about running into him, or others discovering it before she felt able to face them, if they mentioned it to her. But it also meant that there would be no chance to see him, to have coffee or a glass of wine, and try to figure out with him what had happened for him to make such a radical change in his life. He was going to be completely removed, living in Buenos Aires. It sounded sexy and romantic to her. She had no idea how to compete with it and knew she couldn't.

She felt as though she had lost him from the moment he'd told her about it, when in fact she had lost him months before. It made her feel unattractive as a woman, and frightened of the future. She had her job and some of the money her mother had left her, which she had invested carefully when her mother died, but there wasn't much left nearly thirty years later. She was financially dependent on Charles, who had more money than she did, from his family, the trust they had set up for him and his brothers, and his job. He earned more than she did. She was sure he would provide for her. But what if he decided to stay in South America and give up his job? He was close enough to retirement age that he might opt for that, or maybe he would transfer to the HRK office in Buenos Aires where Roberto worked. She might never see him again after he left. And what if something happened to her or she got sick? She had always assumed Charles would be there, and now he wouldn't. Who would be? Her children were young and busy and lived in other cities. She would be all alone now, and Charles would be with Roberto. It made her feel panicked. She had no idea what Charles's plans were, since he didn't know them himself. But she felt as though she was standing on shifting sands, emotionally and financially, which was the reality she had to face now.

They had sworn to each other years before that they would never get divorced. Whatever happened, they would work it out, for their children's sake and their own. Neither of them wanted to be divorced. What had happened to that? He seemed to have forgotten it entirely. And how could she ever take him back now, if he decided Roberto wasn't his future after all, and only a time-out? It would be a lot to ask of her, after everything he was changing now. She couldn't see the future at all anymore. All she saw ahead of her was a thick fog enveloping everything that had been their life.

She was so profoundly shocked she wasn't even sure she missed him. He emailed and texted her a few times to see how she was, but he didn't call. And what was she supposed to say? That she was fine? And everything was great? She could hardly concentrate on her work, and she couldn't sleep at night. She lay awake every night worrying about the future, and examining the past, like a film she kept running to see where the initial flaw was, what mistake she had made that had caused their life to go off the rails. She didn't know what she could have done differently. She thought of all the weekends when she had worn old sweaters and torn jeans, when she didn't wear makeup and barely combed her hair. It was a relief on the weekend not to make the effort, but even she realized that it took more than ratty sweaters and twenty-five years of bad hair days to make your husband fall in love with a man.

She was worried too about how her children would react. She wondered if they would be sympathetic to him, or furious and feel betrayed. She wasn't sure how she felt, let alone able to predict how her children would feel, and they would have little time to adjust. By the time Charles told them during the Christmas holidays, he would be leaving for Buenos Aires in a week. Oona thought his timing was a mistake, but he insisted that he didn't want to ruin Christmas for them. He wanted to leave them their illusions until after Christmas Day.

The holidays seemed irrelevant to her now, and she suspected they would to Will and Meghan as well. Like the house she had rented for their anniversary, it was the last thing on her mind. She had already paid for it so she couldn't back out. There was no cancellation policy that applied. There hadn't been an earthquake that caused the house to fall down, a flood that had washed it away, a war that would stop them from coming, or a terminal illness in her family. It felt as though her life had been hit by a bomb, but nothing that would convince the owners of the house in France to return her money. She didn't even try. And she didn't have the energy for a fight.

Oona continued going to conferences at the office, completing year-end reports, and meeting with authors. She countersigned contracts for one of the firm's major authors. She went through the motions of everything she had to do, but there was a feeling of unreality about everything she touched. She barely ate at night when she went home. It was as though all the color had gone out of her life when Charles moved out, and her life had suddenly switched to black and white. He wasn't an exciting person and never had been. But he had been solid and steady, and she had always known that she could count on him. And now she couldn't anymore. He suddenly belonged to someone else, and the only role she had was of the wife he didn't want. He tried to explain to her by email that he still loved her, but she found that impossible to believe now.

She didn't call anyone or tell a friend. It was so huge that she couldn't find the words or the courage to explain it to someone else and didn't want to. She needed time to herself to get used to the idea. She didn't tell anyone at work what had happened. She made it a policy not to talk about her personal life, and her separation was beyond the scope of the relationships she had at work. She was on good terms with all of her employees, and with her superiors in the parent company, but Charles had been her confidant and best friend, and it was too humiliating to tell anyone what had happened. She wondered what he had told his brothers. She asked right after he moved out and he said he hadn't told them yet. She wondered if he would. They were very conservative, traditional people. She couldn't imagine them being warm and supportive of the changes he was making in his life. Oona had never felt close to them. They had always treated her as an appendage of Charles, not a separate person. She had no deep relationship with them.

With their obsession about money, they had never been impressed with her genteel intellectual job, running a tiny imprint of a bigger house. It wasn't something they understood, and they openly disapproved of Meghan's aspirations to work for a foundation in Africa and thought she should get a "real" job. Will's position at Google was more understandable.

Oona had no family of her own, as the only child of only children who had died young. She had no living relatives except her children and Charles, and she felt the lack of an adult support system now. She was close to one of her colleagues at Hargrove Publishing, who ran a division of the company focused on self-help books and nonfiction, but she was too ashamed of what had happened to talk to her about it, or it was too soon. She wasn't ready to discuss with anyone the fact that Charles had left her, let alone for a man. She felt like an epic failure as a wife. It was hard to see it any other way, and she wasn't willing to demonize Charles. It wasn't his fault if it turned out now that he was gay. She just wished he had come to the realization earlier, or maybe it was better that he hadn't. At least Meghan and Will had had a traditional father until they were adults. She wondered if they were of a generation that would fully accept his change of heart. She knew that many of their friends accepted homosexuality as just one variety of the norm, but she wasn't sure if that included, or would include, their father as part of that trend. She vaguely remembered it happening to one of their friends in high school, and she knew some of their friends were gay, but she suspected that his leaving New York and his job too would compound the issue in their eyes. She was afraid they would view it as an abandonment, which was what it felt like to her. Wherever Charles chose to live now, her life had flipped over entirely. No matter what Charles said about not being sure, and needing to "figure it out," Oona knew that they could never put their marriage back together after something like this. It was over for them, and she was trying to adjust to the idea. She was still struggling with it when he dropped a suitcase off the morning that Will was due back in New York, and Meghan was coming up from Washington by train, three days before Christmas. Oona told him to leave his bag in the guest room, and Charles looked surprised.

"How are we going to explain that to the kids?" She thought he looked pathetic when she answered him. Occasionally she wondered if he had lost his mind.

"We can tell them you're in the middle of a big international deal and getting calls from all over the world at all hours, and you don't want to wake me," she said with an irritated expression. "You didn't think you were going to sleep in our room, did you?" she asked him.

"I didn't know what you'd want to say to the kids." He looked sheepish. It was an awkward situation for both of them, and he felt guilty just being there, but he wanted to spend the holiday with his kids. Roberto was spending Christmas with friends in Connecticut, and he understood that Charles needed this time with his family, so he could explain things to his children. He didn't consider Oona a threat. Charles had told him that he hadn't been in love with her for years, and Roberto believed him. It had the ring of truth.

"When are you planning to tell them?" she asked him. She wanted to be on hand to pick up the pieces afterward, but not be present when he told them. She had already made that clear. He'd had his last day in the office two days before, and he'd be working from the Buenos Aires office three or four days a week.

"The morning after Christmas," he said solemnly. Oona wondered if it was worth the charade before that. It was going to be a Christmas they would always remember whatever day he did it, and they weren't children anymore. The holiday would be ruined for them as soon as he told them his big news and his plans.

"I'm late for a meeting," she said, and left for the office a few minutes later. They had their big office Christmas party that day, and she put a good face on it for her staff. She was standing alone for a few minutes, surveying the group, when her friend Gail Baldwin came over and stood next to her.

"Where've you been hiding out? I haven't seen you in weeks."

"I've been here, just busy with year-end reports."

"I haven't finished mine yet," Gail said with a groan. She was five years older than Oona but looked considerably older with short gray hair and a lined face. She'd been divorced for twenty years and didn't have kids. The division she ran at Hargrove was bigger and more stressful than Oona's lofty elite world of literary authors. They had talent, but were not big moneymakers for the house, selling in small quantities. Gail's authors wrote nonfiction and self-help, which were more commercially viable, and it was an important division. Gail claimed that most of them were crazy, and vegans. "Are you okay?" she asked Oona. She knew her well and something seemed off to her. Oona looked thin and pale, with a distracted expression, and a vague look in her eyes.

"Yeah, pretty much." But Gail could tell she was lying and didn't want to press her. She seemed tired and stressed, usually Oona was much more cheerful. She loved her job and the books that they published. "The kids okay?"

"They're great, coming home tonight." She usually looked happier when she said it. Oona wasn't ready to tell her about the separation yet. She didn't want to deal with people's reactions, even Gail's, especially their sympathy about a possible divorce, which seemed inevitable to Oona. "What are you doing for Christmas?"

"I'm spending it with my mother in Vermont. My brother and sister couldn't do it this year, so it's my turn. Have you heard the rumors around the office by the way?" Gail always knew the inside dirt before anyone else did. Usually Oona was more interested, but today she wasn't. Her own news was more than enough for now, but she pretended to be interested so as not to disappoint Gail. "It hasn't been confirmed yet, but apparently, we're buying Shipsted and Breck. They haven't closed the deal yet, but they're close. I heard it from Marty's assistant. She would know, she knows everything that happens up there." Martin Grass was the CEO. Gail had myriad sources and kept her ear to the ground. She loved knowing all the gossip first and was a great source for Oona.

"What will that mean for us?" Oona asked, mildly concerned.

"Nothing for you. Your imprint is the Great Untouchable, it's iconic, you provide the literary decorum around here. I'm out here among the masses with cookbooks and how to survive menopause."

"There's a need for both," Oona reassured her with a tired smile. She still wasn't sleeping since Charles had moved out, and she was exhausted, almost too much so to worry about the acquisition of another house, which normally would have been of great interest to her.

"We haven't had a big hit in a while. We lost the auction on the last one. I guess they were saving their money to buy S and B. It could mean that about half of us get fired, if it goes through," Gail said.

"Terrific. Merry Christmas to you too. And I'm no safer than you are. We probably make less on all my books than one of yours on do-it-yourself carpentry and how to build your own deck."

"You give us class and literary dignity. Most of my authors write one book and they're done, and if they have a big one, their next one is a flop. What comes after solar panels and a guide to total hip replacement? Or the gourmet side of vegan cuisine?" Gail had no pretensions about the books she published, but she chose them well, they sold incredibly, and they stayed on the bestseller lists for months.

"You've been here longer than anyone else, and you know non-fiction better than anyone in the house," Oona said with a smile.

"That's no guarantee of safe passage these days. It's all about the bottom line. You've got a string of high-end literary successes that win awards to show them. Mine come and go like the wind. It's going to make everyone nervous, that's for sure. They'll have about twice as many people as they need, so heads will be rolling if it goes through."

"When will they know?" It was one more thing to worry about, and Charles's departure was enough for the moment.

"I think they're going to announce it in January, from what Chrystal says. Heads won't start rolling until the spring. But you'll be fine," Gail said again. Two of their coworkers joined them then, they changed the subject, and Oona left half an hour later. She wanted to get home before the kids. She gave Gail a hug and wished her a merry Christmas, and they promised to have lunch to catch up when Gail got back from Vermont. Oona could tell her about the separation then, if she felt up to it. It would seem more real after Charles left New York. For now, it still felt like a bad dream she'd had and would wake up from. But there was no waking up from the reality of Charles being in love with Roberto.

Meghan arrived at their building in the East Seventies by cab, just as Oona's pulled up. She was struggling to get her suitcases, two tennis rackets, some cartons, and a guitar out of the cab, and the doorman and her mother helped her. She had emptied her apartment in Washington and was moving home until she found a job.

"I should have rented a van and driven home," Meghan said, as Oona grabbed the tennis rackets and the guitar, and they got all of it into the elevator and went upstairs. Charles helped them when they got into the apartment and looked happy to see his daughter. And she was happy to see him. He helped carry her suitcases to her room, which led them past the guest room, and she commented as she walked by. The door was open and she saw the suitcase standing next to the bed.

"Who's staying in the guest room?" she asked.

"I am, we're closing a deal with a big new client in Europe, and I have to be available by phone at all hours, and your mother didn't want me keeping her up all night," Charles said.

"Cool," Meghan said, as he set down her bag in her room, and she looked around, happy to be home, and then they both went into the kitchen, where Oona was organizing dinner. Will arrived half an hour later and the apartment felt full and happy and alive. They all admired the Christmas tree Oona had set up in the living room and decorated with a heavy heart. She hated pretending to Will and Meghan that everything was normal, when it wasn't, but it was the way Charles wanted to do it, and she acceded to his wishes, although she could guess that the children would object to having been lied to, but he would have to deal with it when he told them. This was his show now, and she would be there to console them after he left.

Dinner went smoothly that night, Will and Meghan were happy to be home, and their parents were delighted to see them. They all went to their rooms after dinner, the kids to call their friends, Oona to try to relax in the awkward situation, and Charles to the guest room, supposedly to answer emails. The next day, they all had errands to do, the kids had friends to see and last-minute Christmas gifts to buy, and that night both Will and Meghan went out, since the next day was Christmas Eve and they'd be together.

Oona did her best to avoid Charles and stayed in her room most of the time, and Charles was putting on a convincing act of being jovial with the kids. Oona had a splitting headache that night and went to bed.

Their usual caterers made Christmas Eve dinner, and they went to midnight mass afterward as they always did. Instead of putting on Christmas carols and sitting in the living room with the tree lit after mass, Oona made a discreet exit to her room, leaving Charles to hang out with the kids in the kitchen. Meghan stopped in to see her mother on the way to her room to go to bed.

"Are you awake?" she whispered from the door, and Oona smiled at her from the bed. The lights were still on. "You okay, Mom?" She nodded, but the lies and forced gaiety were getting to her.

"I'm just tired, it's been a long week at work." Meghan nodded and went to bed a few minutes later, stopping in to see her brother on the way to her room. He was talking to his girlfriend in California, so Meghan left, and had the gnawing impression that something was wrong, but clearly whatever it was her mother didn't want to talk about it. She wondered if her parents had had a fight.

But Christmas Day seemed almost normal. Oona and Charles played their parts well, everyone loved their gifts, the meal was delicious, and they all went to bed early that night.

The next morning, Oona made a point of getting in and out of the kitchen early and went back to her room with a cup of coffee, intending to stay there while Charles spoke to Meghan and Will after breakfast.

When they both showed up in the kitchen, he had coffee and cinnamon buns ready for them, and they smelled delicious.

"Where's Mom?" Meghan asked. Oona usually made them waffles the morning after Christmas, and there was no sign of her. "Is she sick? She looked really tired last night." Their father was quiet for a minute, and decided that it was time to dive in. He couldn't put it off any longer.

He told them about Roberto, and that he had had to make a hard decision. He knew it would be startling news to them, but he hoped for their support. Then he told them that he was taking a sabbatical, while working part-time from the agency's office in Buenos Aires, and he planned to be there for six months. There was dead silence in the kitchen after he said it, and Charles felt sick when he saw that Will was crying.

"You're *leaving*?" Meghan said with a look of disbelief. "After you tell us you're gay, and you're having a relationship with a man. Are you divorcing Mom?" She was too hurt and angry to even cry, and Will hadn't said a word. He wiped his eyes on his sleeve and waited for his father's answer.

"No, your mom has very kindly agreed to wait while I'm gone, and we'll see where things stand when I get back. She's been amazing about it."

"Have you looked at her lately, Dad? She looks terrible, she looks sick and like she's lost ten pounds since Thanksgiving," and now Meghan knew why. "Why are you leaving now?" She didn't even address the stunning news that he was gay. His imminent departure for six months seemed more pressing. The rest could wait.

"Because Roberto's visa is expiring and we want to be together to figure things out," he said, and it sounded weak even to him.

"Who do you care about, Dad? Some guy you're having sex with, or your wife and kids? You owe Mom more than that. And what about us? Are you going to come back and see us?" Meghan was holding his feet to the fire.

"You can come and see us whenever you want," he said. "I'd like you to meet him, before we go." Will silently shook his head with a dark look at his father and Meghan spoke for them both.

"I don't want to meet him. This isn't about him, it's about us. You're just walking out on everything. Mom, us, your job, your marriage. You're nearly sixty years old. How can you suddenly decide you're gay now?" All the cards were on the table, and Meghan didn't like the hand they'd been dealt. She was losing respect for him by the minute, not for his sexual orientation, which came as a surprise to all of them, but for the way he was handling his exit, running off to South America with his boyfriend. It was the most selfish thing she'd ever heard. "Don't you think you owe it to us to stick around, at least for Mom? You just made a huge announcement that you're gay, and now you're *leaving*?"

"Your mom understands the situation, and it will be better for us to be apart. And I need some time off from my job while I make this adjustment. I can handle some of it from Buenos Aires, and they'll have to manage the rest without me. After ten years with the firm, I'm entitled to a sabbatical. It's in my contract," he said defensively. "Will is in San Francisco, and you want to go to Africa as soon as you find a job you like. My staying in New York won't change anything for you."

"No, but maybe it would for Mom. What is she supposed to do now while you 'figure out your life with Alberto,' or whatever his name is." She sounded strident as she confronted him, and it was painful but he knew he had to endure it. He hadn't expected her to be as angry as she was. She was livid on behalf of her mother, herself, and her brother.

"His name is Roberto. I offered her a divorce if she wants one. She doesn't."

"She's probably too shocked to know what she wants," Meghan guessed accurately.

"We can figure all that out later. Roberto will get his visa back in six months. We'll come back to New York then."

"And what is she going to tell people in the meantime?"

"That's up to her," he said quietly. "This is hard for both of us. We're your parents and we love you, but we both have a right to be happy. This is what I need to be happy right now. I'm older than your mother, and I have a right to happiness in my life before I'm too old to enjoy it," he said, trying to convince her.

"How old is he?" she asked him. He hadn't told them yet. She didn't want to sound critical of his being gay, but Will looked devastated.

"He's thirty-four, and a very responsible person. We didn't set out to destroy this family. It's a hard situation for all of us."

"It sure is," she said, glancing at her brother. "You're going off in pursuit of *your* happiness, and you're leaving Mom here to deal with it alone." He couldn't deny it and didn't answer her. Will looked at him as though his best friend had just died.

"Did you always know you were gay, Dad?" Will asked him, all his illusions about his father shattered.

"No, son, I didn't. I knew it after I began to care for Roberto. I couldn't stop it. I knew then that I couldn't stay with your mom and be dishonest with her about it. I've been wrestling with this for a little over a year. The last thing I wanted to do was hurt her, or either of you, but it is what it is. I think it's something that has lain dormant in me for a long time. I know what I'm doing is right."

"For *you*," Meghan said angrily, "not for the rest of us. You couldn't just stick with what you were doing for the rest of your life? Why do you have to make this enormous change now?"

"I can't lie about who I am," Charles said firmly. "Your mom is younger than I am. If this is the way things work out, she can meet someone else." He made it sound so simple, but it wasn't.

"That's up to me to decide, not you," Oona said in a strong voice. She had walked into the kitchen, and they hadn't seen her. "So I guess you both know what's happening now. And I want to tell you both that I'll be fine," she said, looking at her son and daughter. "I'm as sad about it as you are, but if this is what has to be, and what your father needs, we'll all get through it, and be okay. Sometimes you just can't stop the way destiny works out. We love each other," she said to her children, not her husband, "and I know your dad loves you too, even if it doesn't feel that way right now. There are two issues here. The first is what he's discovered about himself. That we have to respect. He didn't choose it, he found out something important about himself that he couldn't ignore. And the other issue is his going to Argentina for six months. He had a choice about that, but not about his sexual orientation."

"I think it's disgusting that you're just dumping us and going to Argentina," Meghan said to him directly. She had voiced her feelings throughout the conversation with him. Will was deathly pale, and tears kept springing to his eyes faster than he could wipe them away.

"Six months isn't a long time," Charles said softly. "I need this time to find myself," he said. "And you'll both be busy and away. It's up to your mom and me to figure out what to do about our marriage and when."

"I'd still like to go to France with both of you, the way we planned," Oona said to her children. "We have the house for a month, we might as well use it," she said sadly. "And it'll be good for us to get away after all this upheaval."

"I can't take a month off," Will responded immediately. "I asked for a week. I can stay for ten days, and then I have to get back."

"I won't know until I find a job," Meghan added. "But you can stay in France if you want to, Mom. I'll stay as long as I can." She wanted to be there for her mother now. She thought that what her father was doing, just walking out and leaving with his new love for six months, was despicable, and would have been even if it was a woman. It was all about him. She wondered if he had always been that way and their mother had covered for him. He wasn't even apologetic about leaving. He was defensive about it and fighting for his own happiness, regardless of how they or their mother felt.

Will stood up then and said he had to meet a friend. He grabbed a tissue and blew his nose. He looked at his father. "Will we see you again before you go?"

"I'm going to leave the apartment now, and I'll come back to say goodbye to both of you, and if you need to talk before that, you can call me. I'm here for you until I leave. I'm in New York for another six days. Roberto's visa expires on January second." They both nodded their understanding, and Will left the room to get his jacket and was back a minute later and looked at his mother.

"Can I bring Heather to France, Mom? I'd really like to."

She nodded without hesitating. She knew she had to be flexible now, for their sakes. They had had a hard blow, with their father telling them that he was gay, especially Will. And on top of it, was moving to another country with his lover for six months. "You can bring her," Oona confirmed. Meghan didn't have a boyfriend. She hadn't had a serious man in her life in Washington, and she was planning to go far away for a long time. She didn't want to be tied down to a long-distance relationship and had been careful not to get serious about anyone.

"I'm sorry I'm not going with you," Charles said softly.

"No, you're not." Meghan looked at him dead in the eye when she said it. "You're doing exactly what you want to do." She hated him on her mother's behalf. And Oona realized how odd it was that she didn't. She didn't hate him, she didn't feel anything for him, except pity. He was a weak, confused man, who was making selfish decisions that she knew would hurt their children, but she couldn't stop him and she didn't try to. She would do her best to give them the support they needed, and they would have to make their peace with it over time. Charles would have to live with the consequences of his actions. She couldn't protect him this time and had no desire to. He had made his plans with Roberto, without consulting her, and with total disregard of how it would affect his children. She wondered if he really would be happy now, and when he left the apartment, shortly after their children left together, she realized that she didn't care how Charles felt now. It was over for her. Whatever she had felt for him for twenty-five years was dead. She could have still loved him, knowing he was gay. But not with his selfish indifference to his children's feelings. They needed time with him now, to adjust to the situation. Instead he was running away to play with his boyfriend. She had lost all respect for him as a father, and as a man, whatever his sexual orientation. It was all about him, and she realized now it always had been. She could see it clearly now.

Chapter 3

Meghan came back to the apartment a few hours later. She had gone to see a friend. She came to find her mother in her study, and sat down heavily in a chair. She looked exhausted. They all did. It had been a shocking morning for her and Will, and Oona was worried about them. She had been worried about how they would take it, and they had weathered it better than she'd feared. The part that made Charles look bad, and made him seem selfish and heartless, was his running off to Argentina with his new love, with seemingly very little concern for his kids and how they felt. In his mind, they were adults now, and he had a right to his new life, and expected them to understand and even be supportive. It was too much for him to ask, especially of his children.

"Wow, that was quite a morning," Meghan said. "I never could have guessed that. I didn't see it coming. He blindsided us. Poor Will was a mess. I can live with finding out Dad is gay. It's a lot harder for Will. Dad is his role model and idol. I think his running away with his boyfriend is shitty. He should stick around for your sake at least."

"For me, maybe it's better this way," Oona said quietly. "I would hate to run into them somewhere. At least I won't have to worry about that."

"Are you going to divorce him, Mom?"

"I don't know . . . maybe . . . probably, I guess. I'm not ready for that yet. But I don't think he'll come back from what he discovered about himself. I don't think we could ever make our marriage work again. It's less shocking for me than it is for you right now. I've known for a month. He told me the night you both left after Thanksgiving." She crossed the room to hug her daughter and sat down in the big cozy chair next to her.

"Why didn't you tell us?" Meghan asked her, feeling betrayed and disappointed by her father.

"I thought he had a right to tell you himself."

"I nearly fell out of my chair when he said it," Meghan admitted. "I guess shit like this happens, I just never thought it would happen to us."

"Neither did I." Oona smiled at her. "We'll be okay. He'll come back to New York eventually, with or without Roberto, and you'll be able to see him whenever you want."

"I don't want to meet Roberto," Meghan said angrily.

"You may feel differently in a few months, if he's still around. I hope he realizes how much your father has given up to be with him—our marriage, and possibly the respect of his kids, given how he handled it. He's stepping aside from his job while he's in Argentina. He told them he'd go into the office there. I doubt that he'll ever make CEO now. Maybe he doesn't care anymore. He's leaving them in the lurch. That won't sit well. He's putting everything on the line. He must really love Roberto. I don't think he would ever have done all this for me." It was a harsh realization. He was desperate to leave with Roberto now, and pursue the path he was on. He had discovered passion late in the day. It was nothing like the relationship Oona had had with him. It had never been feverish and urgent like this, or even very sexual. The sex had been satisfying enough, but never exciting.

Meghan and Oona spent the afternoon together and had dinner in the kitchen. Will had texted both of them that he would be home late.

Oona waited up for him to make sure he was all right, after his father's revelations. She heard him come in, and Meghan was still awake. He fumbled at the lock with his key, and Oona let him in. He was dead drunk, barely able to stand up, and she helped him to his room as he mumbled that his father was a jerk. Meghan came out of her room to help, and they got him onto his bed, took off the boots he was wearing, and left his clothes on. It would have been too hard to undress him in the state he was in. Oona lovingly covered him with a blanket and left a dim light on so he could find his way to the bathroom if he needed to. He was passed out cold before they left the room, and he looked like he'd had a rough night. At least no harm had come to him, and he was home. Meghan kissed her mother good night, and they went to their rooms, and lay in their respective beds, thinking about the day, and Charles's admissions to his children. Oona wondered if he had any regrets. He hadn't communicated with her after he left. Whatever comfort he needed now he would get from the man in his life and not from her. Her job as his wife was over. He belonged to Roberto now, and had for the past year.

Charles came to say goodbye to Will and Meghan four days later, before Will went back to California to spend New Year's Eve with Heather. He was relieved to leave and get back to her. He needed more right now than his mother or sister could give him. He wanted to sink into Heather's arms, and forget everything that had happened in New York. Heather could give him what comfort he needed better than his mother. Every time he looked at his mother, he could see the pain in her eyes. She was a strong woman and wanted to help them. But Will hated his father every time he saw the devastation on Oona's face. He had told Heather about the trip to France in February, and she was excited to go. He was going as a gesture of support for his mother, not because he wanted to. He was doing it for her. And having Heather with him would make it more fun for him.

Charles's visit to say goodbye to them was short and awkward. He and Will shook hands, and he hugged Meghan, and he reminded both of them that they could reach him in Argentina on his American cell phone. Roberto had sublet his apartment for the year he was in New York, and it had been recently vacated. They would be living there. It was a simpler life than Charles was used to, and he said he didn't care. Roberto said the apartment was small, in a slightly rundown residential neighborhood.

Oona was out when Charles came to see them, and she preferred it that way. She had made a point of not being there. She didn't need to say goodbye to him—they had said everything that needed to be said. He had emailed her to tell her he was going to put a generous amount in her bank account every month and told her to spend what she needed. He didn't want to make any formal financial arrangements with her, as that would make it seem too final. In the back of his mind, he thought he could come back if he wanted to. Oona doubted that he would, but she already knew she wouldn't let him come back to her. She wasn't ready to file for divorce, but she knew she would when she was ready to, whenever that was. Until then, she had her own salary, and whatever he gave her. All she needed now was to find her way to solid ground again. She felt as though the world had collapsed under her feet.

She told Gail about the separation when she went back to work after New Year. Gail was shocked when she told her. She had always been sure that their marriage was rock solid and would last forever.

"I thought so too," Oona said with a sigh, but she looked better than she had before Christmas. She felt more like herself again. It was beginning to sink in. "If you had told me he would figure out that he was gay and fall in love with a man, I would never have believed you," Oona said.

"I guess it happens that way sometimes," Gail said, still stunned by everything Oona had told her.

Oona's news was rapidly eclipsed by the news the next day that the acquisition of Shipsted and Breck publishers by Hargrove was definite. The deal had been signed. They would be merging the two publishing houses in the next two months, and by March, they would be making room for new members of the staff, inherited from S&B. It was inevitable that some members of the old Hargrove staff would have to go, but Oona was assured by the CEO that her imprint was safe, as an iconic part of the house they were proud of, just as Gail had said.

"I'm glad I'll be away when the initial transitions start to happen. Everyone is going to be panicked. I'll be in France then, and by a month later when I get back, things should have settled down a little."

"Yeah, if I haven't been fired by then," Gail said glumly.

"You're as safe as I am," Oona reassured her. It was anyone's guess who would have to go, but at least both of them were secure in their jobs. A merger always meant a lot of management and policy changes, which would take months for operations to run smoothly again. They weren't looking forward to it.

At the end of January, Meghan secured the job of her dreams with a paid internship in the children's section of a refugee camp in Kakuma, Kenya. They had a population of close to two hundred thousand refugees in the camp, mostly Ethiopians and Somalis, many of them children. They were desperate for more workers at the camp. They were willing to wait for her until the end of February. She had to start getting her vaccinations immediately, and she would be trained on the ground when she got there. She was going to spend a week with her mother at the house in France, and fly straight from there to Nairobi, and then by chartered flight to Kakuma. Meghan was thrilled with the job they described. It was exactly what she wanted. The United Nations Refugee Agency, where she had applied, had hired her. Oona was happy for her but concerned for her safety. They told Meghan that conditions there were relatively safe for the workers. And the camp workers' housing areas were well guarded, and respected by the local government. That reassured Oona somewhat, and Meghan couldn't wait to go after her week in France.

Meghan and Will had both heard from their father by then. It was summer in Argentina, and he loved it. Meghan told him about the job in an email and he congratulated her and told her he was very proud of her. The words felt empty to her. He seemed like a phantom father to her now. He was pursuing his own dreams, and not involved in her life. He was too far away to call regularly, and too self-involved. It was all about him.

They were reading about a serious flu epidemic in China by then, but there was no sign of it in Africa, so Meghan wasn't concerned. It appeared to be contained in China.

By the time Oona flew to France on Valentine's Day, there were rumors of cases of the flu from China appearing in Italy, around Milan, among Chinese factory workers who had flown to China, and specifically Wuhan, to celebrate Chinese New Year. But there were only ten cases in France, all people who had been to China, or had been in contact with them. The cases in France had been detected three weeks before, and were in Bordeaux, only one in Paris, and a few in the Haute-Savoie. Air France had suspended all flights to Mainland China two weeks earlier, except for a single daily flight to Beijing and Shanghai, and they had stopped all service to Wuhan, the hub of the flu epidemic in China, three weeks before Oona flew to France. The situation appeared to be under control and Oona wasn't worried. China was a long way away, and ten cases of Covid-19 did not constitute an epidemic in France.

Meghan and Will would be joining her a week later, and Oona was excited to see the house she had rented for a month. She hoped it would be as beautiful as it was in the photographs. It had a fascinating history and had been built for the favorite mistress of the French king whose country château was nearby, in Milly-la-Forêt, an hour outside Paris. There were said to be underground tunnels leading directly to the château when the house was built. The king's château had been burned and destroyed during the French Revolution, but the mistress's house, named "La Belle Florence" after her, was still intact, 230 years later, and full of charm. The young mistress was said to have died a mysterious death, and the house had been in the hands of numerous owners in the two centuries since it was built.

La Belle Florence was a 230-year-old very large house with eight main bedrooms, but it was not unmanageably large and had looked gracious and elegant in the photographs. It had been impeccably restored with all modern conveniences and beautifully decorated by the family in Hong Kong that currently owned it, but seldom used it, and rented the property out to carefully screened renters. The month there had been Oona's anniversary gift to Charles, and he had been thrilled when she told him about it. That was irrelevant now. After the shock of the last three months, being there alone didn't seem daunting to her now. She needed the break and wanted to get away. There was a definite feminine feel to it, which the current owners had maintained. And the broker had told her that there were several fairly large châteaux in the area, but they were not related to the mistress's house. One of the châteaux now belonged to a famous British film producer. He lent it to friends occasionally. By comparison, the mistress's house that Oona had rented looked like a little jewel. The week she was planning to spend there with her children would be the last time the three of them would be together for many months, since after that Will would be in San Francisco, Meghan in Africa, and Oona in New York. Charles was in Argentina now. They were spread all over the world. She wanted everything about Will and Meghan's stay to be perfect, to add a happy memory to the recent unhappy ones that she knew had marked both her children, just as the end of her twenty-five-year marriage had marked her. They needed some good times now to boost their spirits and put balm on the wounds inflicted by Charles.

Oona was planning to spend the first week there getting settled and exploring the area, so she would know where to take Meghan, Will, and Heather when they arrived. There were some quaint small restaurants in the area, a famous church, and another well-known château farther away with exceptionally beautiful gardens. And La Belle Florence had exquisite gardens as well. It was still winter, but there were walks one could take on the grounds. Oona had been assured that the house was well heated. There was a daily housekeeper who came with the house, and they were going to try the local bistros. The young people were only staying for a week, and Oona would have two weeks there alone after they left. It was only an hour outside Paris, and there was a car service available if they wanted to go into the city, which she was more likely to do after they left, since Will didn't enjoy shopping or museums, and Meghan was going to a place where she would wear only rough clothes for the next year, so she had nothing to shop for. Oona was planning to save her day trip to Paris for when she was alone. It was mainly a time for the family to enjoy being together, and she was glad they were willing to come. And there was plenty to see in the area of historical interest to keep them busy.

She had a few emails from Charles the first week she was in France, telling her he was sorry he wasn't there. It seemed simpler not to respond, since his saying that seemed hypocritical in the circumstances. She was sure he had no regrets, and if he did, she didn't want to know about them.

As soon as Oona saw the house, she had none herself. It was even more beautiful than the photographs she had seen when she rented it. It was in immaculate condition, and all the historical details had been respected and restored according to the original plans. The Hong Kong family and their architects and decorators had done a beautiful job with it. It was an elegant home, in the midst of lush countryside despite the winter landscape. The gardens were impeccably kept by a fleet of gardeners, and there were stables with half a dozen horses if she wanted to ride. She knew that Will and Meghan would enjoy the horses. The bedrooms were big and comfortable. The kitchen looked antique but was in fact ultramodern, and the house had been decorated with high-quality furniture of the period. She loved everything about the house and smiled broadly as she walked from room to room. She couldn't wait for her children to see it. She told Meghan about it on the phone.

"It is gorgeous," Oona said, delighted after she had completed her tour of the house and the grounds. The broker had been there to meet her and show her everything—there was even an excellent stereo system, and a movie theater in the basement. She tried not to think about it, but Charles would have loved it. There was a well-stocked wine cellar for her use, with a locked section with the owner's exceptional wines. But what was there was more than adequate for her, and she had no one to entertain there after her children left.

She described it all to Meghan, who was happy to hear her mother so enthusiastic. She had facetimed Meghan to show her some of the details, and Oona didn't stop smiling for the entire call. She had barely seen her mother for three months, and she sounded like herself again, once she'd seen the house. She looked genuinely happy.

"Be careful while you're there though, Mom," Meghan warned her, "the virus seems to have migrated from China to Europe and is wandering around. They think it's in the States now too. There have been cases in California, brought in by people traveling from Asia, and some cases in New York, possibly from Europe. I heard it on the news this morning."

"There's no one on the property except us, and the housekeeper who comes every day. There are gardeners outside, tending the gardens, which are dormant, and two men in the stable for the horses, but we won't see anyone unless we go to Paris, or some of the local restaurants, which the broker said we should try. Some of them are excellent, but we have everything we need here at the house. We don't have to go out at all if we don't want to."

"It sounds fantastic, Mom." Meghan was happy for her mother, and Oona sent Will a text as soon as she and Meghan hung up. She told him to bring boots he could ride in. She knew he'd love the horses. There was a big swimming pool out of sight as well, and tennis courts. The owners had modernized it in just the right way, unobtrusively, and Oona was surprised they seldom used it, but the broker said they had a larger home in Switzerland as well, which they preferred, a house in London, and an apartment in Paris. She said they had bought La Belle Florence more for its charm and history, which the owner's wife loved, but her husband was happier at their home in Switzerland. The mistress's house was more intimate, but too small for the large entourage the owners traveled with, and there wasn't enough room for their staff, who came from Hong Kong with them in their private jet. It was just an additional home they liked to own but seldom used, and Oona couldn't help thinking how fortunate they were to own something like it. She wished she could stay longer but had to get back to work. She had four weeks off and intended to enjoy every minute.

The housekeeper, Marie, had left dinner for her. There were all the local delicacies. There was an excellent pâté, some sausages, a chicken she had kindly roasted for her, lettuce for a salad, pasta in the cupboard if she wanted it, and local herbs—the area was famous for its aromatic and medicinal herbs. Marie had also left an assortment of fruit juices, local bread, some cheese from a nearby dairy, and an espresso machine Oona wasn't sure how to use, which the broker said made cappuccino. Her children were going to love it, and she couldn't wait for them to come.

By the time they arrived, Oona had explored the area with one of the stable hands to guide her, and he had pointed out all the best places to go and taken her to a local market where she bought all the things she thought Meghan and Will would enjoy. Her French was limited but adequate for her to ask prices and speak to the vendors. The stable hand had given her a map of the area.

They arrived on separate flights from San Francisco and New York, and Meghan was the first to arrive, on an overnight flight that landed her at Charles de Gaulle at seven o'clock in the morning. With the hour's drive after she claimed her luggage, it was nine A.M. when Oona heard the car that she had ordered to pick her up come up the driveway. Meghan was bringing with her everything she needed for Africa packed into an enormous backpack and two big duffel bags. She looked sleepy when she arrived after the night flight and had dozed in the car, and Oona was standing in the driveway to greet her, in a knitted cap, jeans, boots, and a heavy jacket. It was a cold, sunny February morning, and Oona was beaming when she saw her daughter and hugged her as soon as she got out of the car. Meghan hadn't seen her look that happy in months as they walked into the house together and Meghan looked around, stunned by the beautiful rooms that were elegant but warm and inviting. The fabrics were lovely and historically accurate, and the art on the walls was impressive. The housekeeper had lit a fire in the living room for additional warmth, and Oona walked Meghan upstairs to her bedroom, while one of the stable hands brought up her luggage and set it down in the bedroom Oona had chosen for her. It was all done in delicate pink silks with a big down comforter on the four-poster bed. Meghan grinned as soon as she saw it.

"This is amazing. It's even prettier than you said."

"I love it. I want to stay forever," Oona said happily, and showed her the even larger bedroom she had chosen for Will, since he would be sharing it with Heather, and it looked a little more masculine than Meghan's pink room. His had blue and yellow striped satin curtains and upholstery and slightly larger-scale furniture. Meghan went back to her own room to wash her face and hands and take off her jacket, and walked down to the kitchen with her mother, where Marie, the friendly housekeeper who spoke a little English, had coffee ready for them, and a basket of warm croissants and local pastries, with a bowl of fresh fruit on the table.

"You're going to ruin me for life in a refugee camp, Mom," Meghan said with a grin as she sat down at the table, helped herself to a croissant, and sipped the coffee, while Oona had a cappuccino and enjoyed her daughter's company. Will wasn't expected until noon, and after breakfast Oona walked Meghan around the grounds, and they visited the stable before going back to the house.

"This is magical," Meghan said, and Oona agreed with her.

"I was terrified it would turn out to be awful, and we'd hate it here. Now I wish I could stay longer."

"Why don't you, Mom?"

"I can't, especially with the new merger. They're all nervous wrecks at the office. I need to go back and set a good example." Meghan's face clouded as her mother said it.

"It doesn't seem fair that Dad turned your life upside down, and he's going to spend the next six months working part-time in Argentina, going to the office when he feels like it, and you have to go back to work."

"He's on a sabbatical. I'm not," her mother answered. It annoyed Meghan that he had no responsibilities now, and could play around in Argentina with his boyfriend, and her mother had to go back to a job and an empty apartment, with both her children far away. They both knew that Oona was going to be lonely when she went back to New York. She and Charles hadn't spent a lot of time together in recent years, but he was there, someone to come home to, and in her bed every night. He was a live human to talk to, and to be there if she was tired, lonely, or sick. She wouldn't have that now, or even her children in the same city. Oona was acutely aware of it. She hadn't lived alone for twenty-five years, except for the few weeks just now between Thanksgiving and Christmas, until Meghan got home. Now she would be going home to a dark, empty apartment every night. Oona tried not to think about it. She had this exquisite house in the meantime, for the next three weeks, and then real life and the reality of her current situation would hit her. Meghan hated the thought of it for her, and the fact that both she and Will would be so far away. But she knew that Oona was resourceful and not one to feel sorry for herself, and she would keep busy. It seemed so unfair that her mother was going to be alone, and her father would be having all the fun with the romance that hit their life like a bomb. Her mother would be the one to pay the price for it, although she had done nothing wrong. Every time Meghan thought of it, she was furious at her father. He was changing his whole identity at fifty-nine, and her mother had to go on alone, and reinvent her life.

* * *

Will's plane was slightly delayed, and he and Heather arrived at one-thirty, which was four-thirty in the morning for them, but after a look around their bedroom, they were wide awake and sat down to a hearty lunch with Meghan and their mother in the kitchen. The formal dining room had a table that seated twenty, with a beautiful antique crystal chandelier. Heather looked slightly intimidated, but Meghan admitted to her mother later that she liked her more than she'd expected to. She had assumed she would be some pushy woman who was taking advantage of Will, and instead she was a nice girl from Salt Lake City who had gone to UCLA. She seemed very knowledgeable about art, and looked carefully at all the paintings in the house, admiring them, and thanked Oona profusely for allowing her to come. She seemed like a nice person and was crazy about Will, and the three of them went riding that afternoon, while Oona organized dinner.

Heather had brought several books with her about the historical sights to see in the area. She had a long list of châteaux she showed Oona, and they chose Château de la Bonde, a thirteenth-century castle, to visit the next day, and the fifteenth-century covered market in the town square. Supposedly one could find treasures from several centuries there. It was frequented by Parisian antique dealers and sounded like a fun adventure for the four of them. That night, after their long flights the night before, they all went to bed early, and planned to use the movie theater the following night. The owners had an entire library of movies, most of them British, so there were lots of films for them to enjoy.

Oona made breakfast for all of them the next morning, and Château de la Bonde, with two towers and a beautiful stone bridge, was well worth the visit. They had lunch at a local restaurant, and then went on to a nearby antique market they had read about, and they each found something to take home. Meghan discovered some Bakelite jewelry she loved that she could wear on special occasions in Africa, Heather bought a stack of old books, which she collected, and Will was delighted with a nineteenth-century military cap that fit him perfectly. Oona found a set of tortoiseshell toiletry articles for her dressing table at home, and Heather bought a vintage leather jacket. They returned to the house with their treasures, and sat by the fire, drinking cappuccino, which Will had figured out how to make and was delicious. He put some music on the stereo and they all felt at home.

Oona was relieved to see Will back to his old self, despite his father's revelations of two months before. Heather fit in perfectly. She had brought some games with her to add to the party, which they played after dinner, and then went to watch a movie in the very comfortable movie theater. Meghan giggled at how much fun it all was, and Will delighted in telling embarrassing stories about their childhood. Heather came from a family with five children, and said she was enjoying being with Will, Meghan, and Oona. She missed her siblings a lot, living in San Francisco, and she said she couldn't believe how lucky she was to be there with Will and his family. She had never been to Europe before, and she'd been reading about French art before the trip. It gave Oona the idea that maybe they should go into the city after all, and she arranged for a car the next day, and asked the car service if they could get them tickets for the Louvre, which they said they would do.

As it turned out, the trip to Paris was one of the high points of their holiday. They started at the Louvre, which thrilled Heather, and she had tears in her eyes when she saw the *Mona Lisa*. Oona treated them to lunch at the Bar Vendôme at The Ritz nearby. They walked around the Place Vendôme, visited the Bon Marché, an elegant department store, and went to the food hall and bought all kinds of things they wanted to eat, and then drove to the Place de la Concorde, and up the Champs-Élysées to the Arc de Triomphe, got out to take some photographs, and drove back to Milly-la-Forêt in time to make dinner with many of the special items they had bought at the Bon Marché. They made a delicious dinner together and sat talking for a long time about other trips they'd taken as children, to England and Italy, and Spain. Oona and Charles had loved traveling with their children, and Heather was in awe of the experiences they had shared. It seemed like part of a different life now that their father had embarked on an entirely new life, which no longer included them. Heather was aware of the drastic changes Will's father had made, and the impact it had on all of them. It was different now, having met Will's mother and sister, and she suddenly realized how deeply it had affected each of them, and not just Will, when his father admitted to being gay and announced that he was moving to Argentina for six months. For the time being at least, he had abandoned all of them for his adventure in Argentina with the man he was in love with. It was a lot for all of them to absorb, and impossible not to feel betrayed. Will had told her that his mother had rented the house in France to celebrate his parents' twenty-fifth anniversary, and now they would probably be getting divorced instead. Heather gave Oona a warm hug that night before they went upstairs and thanked her for including her on their family trip.

"I really like her," Oona commented to Meghan when she came to her bedroom a little while later.

"I do too," Meghan admitted. "I thought I was going to hate her, since he had to transfer at work because of her. But she's nice, and he needs her right now." Their father's change of life had hit him hard, maybe even harder than his sister, because his father had been his role model and hero all his life.

"I like that she's from a big family. She's unassuming and very bright," Oona said of her. "It's too bad he met her now. He's too young to take her too seriously. At twenty-seven, she's closer to settling down than he is at twenty-four. I hope he doesn't get married for a long time. He's too young to think about that now."

"I don't think he is. They're just having a nice time together, and she's been kind to him after the whole mess with Dad." Will had said as much to his sister, and she could see that Heather had a very nurturing side, maybe from being the oldest of five siblings. "I'm glad you let her come, Mom. It means a lot to Will."

"It turned out to be a very different trip from the one I planned, but I'm having a lot of fun with the three of you," Oona said with a gentle smile. She'd had a terrific two days with them so far.

"So am I," Meghan said, hugged her mother and went back to her bedroom. She smiled, looking around the room before she went to sleep. She was going to be living a very different life a week from now, in a dormitory tent at the refugee camp in Kenya.

This was all going to seem like a dream to her then, but in the meantime, they were building another memory for the future, the first one without their father.

In her room, Oona was thinking the same thing. From now on, everything would be "before Charles left" and "after," and for the first time she realized that maybe the life they would lead "after Charles" wouldn't be so bad after all. They were still a family and their stay at the mistress's house would be the first of many new memories. She didn't know when she would be with both her children again, but they were all she needed now. She didn't need a new man in her life, nor want one. Charles had caused her too much pain. Will and Meghan were enough. And for the very first time since Charles had told her he was leaving her, she knew now that she would be fine on her own. She had survived the shock of losing him and she was still whole.

Chapter 4

The eight days that Oona spent with her children in France felt like a longer vacation to all three of them. Each day had its own special quality, its discoveries and joys, funny moments, and laughter. It was the best time she had spent with her children in years, and they thrived on her undivided attention. She realized now that without their father present, both of her children were more relaxed, and that Charles had competed subtly for her attention whenever they were together. She wondered if he was jealous of them, or just more narcissistic than she had recognized. It certainly looked that way now. He had chosen a path and a life that was good for him, with total disregard for how it affected anyone else. Will was still shaken to his core by his father's revelations. It was startling enough that Charles had discovered he was gay, but running off to South America with his lover gave them no time to adjust or have support from him whatsoever. And he contacted them far less than Oona would have expected. It was sink or swim for them now, his way or no way. He was doing what he wanted, but hardly ever checked in with them about their lives. It was as though suddenly he felt young and unencumbered again, with no responsibilities at all. And he was counting on Oona, as he always had, to clean up the debris he had left behind, and cover for him with their children.

She didn't want them any more hurt than they already were, but she was no longer inclined to repair his damage and smooth things over. He needed to do that himself. He paid even less attention to how Oona was feeling now. He sent her the occasional email that sounded drunk and disjointed, sharing with her that he loved his new life of freedom from a regular work schedule, and the burdens of marriage and fatherhood, and then complaining that Roberto's apartment was small and his cleaning woman had stolen money from Charles, and that he missed having Oona to run his life, as a kind of social secretary and majordomo. He talked about what a smooth and efficient house she ran, despite her own career, and said she could give Roberto lessons of how it should be done. Roberto wanted to go out every night, go to gay bars and party, and Charles wanted to stay home. It was the difference between thirty-four and fifty-nine, which Charles didn't seem to understand, and didn't want to. He seemed to be trying to turn Oona into some kind of mother figure, or sister, or confidant he could complain to, while forgetting how completely he had upended her life and absolved himself of any responsibility for it. He sounded like a spoiled young wife, and not a grown man. More and more she was realizing the tasks and burdens she had shouldered, so he didn't have to. They both came home from work at night, Charles usually after dinner with clients, or so he claimed, but he would then expect Oona to console him for whatever had gone wrong in his day, and offer creative solutions, even when her day had been harder than his, and all she wanted to do was lie on the bed and stare at the ceiling and let her mind go blank for a while, not solve his work problems as well as her own.

They had slipped into a routine of camaraderie, and as it turned out, he was having an affair with someone else. She doubted now that he had been out with clients every night and played golf on Saturdays. She suspected now that a good many of those nights had been spent with Roberto, and not with clients at all. He had turned out to be a liar and a cheat as well as confused about his own identity, and irresponsible. There was a lot he would have to do to rebuild his relationship with his children, and Oona wasn't at all sure that he was going to make the effort to do it, although she didn't say it to Will or Meghan. They would have to discover for themselves what kind of man their father was. As for herself, she had the distinct impression that he was trying to keep her on the back burner in case things didn't work out with Roberto. He was young and from a different world, and she wondered if at some point Charles would tell her that he had decided he wasn't gay and would want to come back to her because it was easy, and then lie to her all over again. He had shattered all her illusions about him and their marriage.

Charles's relationship with Roberto had gone on for a year in secret and he had lied to her the entire time. Bailing on his job and his marriage was convenient for him now. If one day he wanted to do an about-face, she suspected that he might want her to be part of that plan, and she was no longer a willing recruit, and nor could she see herself enlisting again. She was surprised by how happy she was without him. More than she had expected to be. She had her children to keep her company, but soon she would be alone. She wasn't looking forward to it.

Being in France gave her some distance from it all, and she felt less abandoned by him, the way she had in the apartment in New York. These were brand-new surroundings in a different place, and she felt liberated. It was an unfamiliar feeling for her, and she liked it. She could understand what he must be feeling with Roberto. Aside from the passion, it was a whole new life they were each embarking on. For Oona, the trip to France was the best thing that had happened to her in years.

On Will, Heather, and Meghan's last night, they went to a well-known restaurant in a nearby village. People came from Paris to have dinner there, and it was only a ten-minute drive for them. The restaurant specialized in seafood, and they all agreed that it was one of the best fish dinners that they had ever eaten. Will had selected a very nice wine. He had become interested in wine since living in California, and frequently went to the Napa Valley to try new ones. He had tried a number of French wines on the trip, and he had discovered some new favorites. Oona had been impressed by his choices, and the knowledge he had acquired.

After dinner, they went home and sat by the fire in the living room, enjoying the atmosphere of the house.

"I think this is one of the best trips we ever had," Will complimented her. He had had a great time with his mother and sister, and exploring the area with Heather, who always had some new fact to share, or a château or a church she thought they should see, and he had enjoyed them all. "We should try to take a trip together this summer. It doesn't have to be as fancy as this. We could go to Tahoe for a few days, or Santa Barbara, or the Napa Valley." And then he remembered that his sister would be away for a year, and it wouldn't be as much fun without her. A year seemed like such a long time, and it did to Oona too. But Meghan was thrilled to be going. Everything about Africa fascinated her. The animals, the game preserves, the wilderness, the people, and the good she could do there.

They stayed up late talking, and Oona hated to think that it was her last night with them for God knew how long. It gave her a little panicky feeling, knowing how far away they'd be, but she was planning to go to California to visit Will at some point in the summer, and he had promised to come to New York if he could, but whenever it was, she knew it wouldn't be soon, and she couldn't put her arms around them on FaceTime or Skype. She knew she would miss them terribly when they left the next day.

It was two in the morning when they all finally retired to their bedrooms. They had to leave by six A.M. to catch their flights to San Francisco and Nairobi, which was the first leg of Meghan's trip to Kakuma, in the northwest of Kenya. They had a long day of travel ahead of them, Meghan even more than Will.

Oona made breakfast for them before they left and stood in the driveway as they drove away with the car service. Meghan and Heather had become good friends by then, and Will was sorry that his sister would be gone for so long. They all promised to text Oona when they arrived at their respective destinations so she'd know they got there safely. She worried about them even though they were grown-up now. They didn't seem so grown-up to her, and the three of them felt closer than ever before, especially since their father had left their inner circle and betrayed them. It had created a tighter bond between them, and Heather had been a warm, easy addition.

The house seemed deadly quiet and sad when Oona came back into it after they left. It was early and she went back to bed. She slept for another two hours and then woke and read the American newspapers online. She saw that the coronavirus was worsening all over the world. In France a group of twenty-five hundred evangelists had congregated in the last week, and more than half had contracted the virus. The word "pandemic" was being used repeatedly. Experts were predicting dire numbers and opinions were varied and contradictory about what to do about it. It was unsettling reading about how quickly it was spreading. But since there was nothing she could do, she decided not to read about it constantly. It was just too upsetting. Hopefully it would turn around soon, although there were apparently thousands dead of the virus in China. She decided not to let it ruin the second half of her vacation, which would already be very different without Will and Meghan, and even Heather. They had added so much joy to the trip, and Oona had to fight waves of loneliness when they were gone. It was inevitable since she was alone. She had to get used to it.

Oona rented a small car for the two weeks after they left, and drove around the countryside and neighboring villages on her own. She didn't go to most restaurants alone, but there were plenty of little bistros where she could go for lunch, where no one would pay any attention to a woman by herself, and she enjoyed watching people. She went back to one of the *brocantes*, which were like giant yard sales, where she'd gone with her children, and found a few more things. It was like a treasure hunt again. She went for long walks, and went riding with one of the stable hands, who showed her the best trails to follow, and made sure that nothing dangerous happened to her. It was a healthy, peaceful two weeks, and it felt wonderful to be in France.

She kept track of the progress of the virus on the news every day or two, and it was worsening everywhere. It seemed hard to believe that it was getting out of control so rapidly. It was like an unseen enemy. In the quiet, bucolic country scene where everything seemed so peaceful, a potential killer was lurking.

It was two days before she was due to leave when the United States and all of Europe reacted to what was now clearly a pandemic, involving every country in the world. The United States called all Americans home, their spouses even if foreign, and holders of green cards, permanent resident cards for foreigners, and closed their borders to everyone else. Europe immediately did the same, closing the Schengen borders—the outer borders of Europe—to anyone outside them, although travel between countries within Europe was allowed. It was a massive recall for everyone to go home. Americans would continue to be allowed to go home at any time, but no one else would be allowed to enter the U.S. after the next thirty-six hours. France closed schools and universities, banned public gatherings, closed all nonessential public places, including all restaurants, cafés, stores, and hair salons, and announced mandatory home lockdown. Only grocery stores and pharmacies remained open. The catch-22 was that travel, particularly air travel, was said to be extremely dangerous. Oona was scheduled to go home anyway, but getting there sounded risky with the Covid numbers rising daily, and airports crowded with people on long lines, waiting up to eight hours to complete the process of reentry into the United States.

She was grateful that Will and Heather had gotten back to San Francisco safely, without incident. And Meghan had arrived in Nairobi and traveled from there to Kakuma, Kenya, with no problem. She had texted her mother as soon as she arrived and was thrilled with her job at the refugee camp. She was still in training for another two weeks but was already responsible for a group of ten little girls, as the assistant to their main caretaker, and she would have a group of her own, when she completed training.

Meanwhile, Oona did not know what to do about her own departure, when France announced the total lockdown. Everything was due to be shut down, offices were to operate remotely, with all employees working from home on their computers, while parents, working from home, were to homeschool their kids until further notice, with teachers conducting remote classes online. The entire country was coming to a dead stop, by order of the French president, whereas the United States was being fragmented by state and city with governors and mayors making the decisions about whether to lock down or not, and to what degree, with a vast divergence and divisiveness from city to city and state to state.

Oona didn't know who to talk to about making the decision to travel or not. Normally, she would have discussed something that serious with Charles, but it didn't feel right to call him. Legally, he was still her husband, but in fact he wasn't, he was Roberto's, or his boyfriend at the very least. She called Will and he agreed that travel was dangerous, and he wasn't keen on the idea of her flying home, potentially with a plane full of people with Covid and air circulating throughout the plane. Most flights were being canceled. Will said that Google had sent them home to work remotely, and their offices were closed. The entire staff was working from their homes. San Francisco was completely shutting down, with only essential workers, those involved in food or medical care, allowed to work at all. No hairdressers, gardeners, restaurants, stores, or anyone nonessential was allowed to work. Will said that everyone had been told to stay home, although New York was still much more open, and the virus was wreaking havoc there.

Oona had also sent a text to Meghan asking her to call. She had to go into Kakuma town to get to a phone, and she told her mother that as there were almost no cases in Africa so far, she felt safer there and she was staying. All her fellow workers had come to that same decision. Staying where they were seemed safer, and all the workers were needed at the refugee camp. And by the time Meghan called her mother, all air travel to and from Kakuma had been canceled indefinitely due to Covid. So Meghan had no way out.

"What if you can't get home later, if the situation gets worse?" Oona asked her.

"It won't, Mom. Americans can always go back to the U.S. If I could get to Nairobi and find a flight, they wouldn't stop us from coming home, but it's too dangerous for me to fly back right now, and there are no flights from here to Nairobi. I'm much safer here. There are plenty of other health risks and diseases here but not Covid. I've been vaccinated for all of them. You're at much higher risk flying home from France than I am here, in Africa." By then, Oona had seen the long lines going through immigration. Reentering the United States, the lines were said to take four to eight hours, with people who might or might not be sick standing in crowded conditions, pressed against each other with no distancing. It didn't look appealing, compared to her peaceful country haven near Milly-la-Forêt outside Paris.

Not knowing who else to call, Oona called Gail, who was always a sensible woman, not given to hysteria or exaggeration.

"How is it there?" Oona asked her.

"I don't know really. The number of new cases is staggering here, and deaths. The ICUs are jammed. They closed the office, the whole building is empty, and we're all going to work from home. Are you coming back?" Gail asked her.

"I haven't decided. I don't even know if I have an option. I'm not in my own home, I'm in a rented house, and my contract ends the day after tomorrow. I have no idea if I can extend my stay, and all the hotels are closed. I may have to fly home, but it's scary as hell from what I've seen on TV. This really feels like a war now, and they're calling everyone back to their home countries. It's the unseen enemy. It seems so peaceful here, but they're shutting everything down, and Paris is completely locked down. All of France is. You can only leave your house with a permission paper, for food, for medical purposes, or to walk your dog."

"Get a dog immediately," Gail advised her, and Oona laughed. Gail always had a way of lightening the moment.

"I don't know what to do," Oona said, worried, "whether to stay or make a run for it to get home. The mobs in the airport look terrifying, and the plane could be dangerous too." She had no one to rush home to, no reason to go back, and if they were all working from home now, she could just as easily work with her computer in France, have Zoom meetings, and use FaceTime and Skype.

"Do you think the owners of the house would let you stay?" Gail asked her.

"I can ask. I don't know if anyone else has rented it after I leave. The owners can't use it. They can't get into Europe from Hong Kong—unless they're at one of their other homes in Europe. According to the realtor, they hardly ever use this one, except to rent it out short-term, like to me. It's the wife's plaything, and her husband thinks it's too small. They have a big family and an enormous staff who travel with them."

"Have you had fun?" Gail asked her, happy to hear from her. It had been a stressful time in New York, worrying about catching the virus, and watching the numbers mount exponentially every day. Gail was lonely in her apartment. She liked going to work every day for social contact. Oona knew she would be just as lonely on her own, without Charles or the children, and her housekeeper probably wouldn't be able to come. It was a lot more pleasant being in the country with the woods and the hills, walks she could take alone, and the horses to ride on sunny days. Spring was starting to peek through the branches, although there was still occasional frost on the ground. She could have gone to the house in the Hamptons, but it always depressed her except in summer. It felt so bleak in winter, unlike France, and all the restaurants and shops would be closed in the Hamptons too. Most of the United States was shutting down.

"It's been wonderful," Oona said warmly to Gail. "I had a great time with the kids. They left two weeks ago. Will is back in San Francisco, working from home—Google's offices are closed too. And Meghan loves her job in Africa. She says it's safer there than it is here. They hardly have any cases—it hasn't really gotten there yet. I even enjoyed being here after they left. I don't feel lonely here. It's just peaceful and rural, an hour out of the city. I've only gone into Paris a couple of times, but everything will be closed now, and we've been ordered to stay home."

"If I were you, I'd try to stay. Nothing's happening here. And it won't make a difference if you do Zoom meetings from France or here, it's all the same. No one will care. It doesn't matter where you are. And why should you take the risk of flying home with no one to come home to?" As usual, Gail made sense, and after they hung up, Oona walked around the house, thinking about it. No one was clamoring for her to go home, and her office was closed. She called the realtor a few minutes later and explained the situation to her. She understood perfectly, and said she'd contact the owners through their office in Hong Kong, if it was open. The owners' very efficient secretary would know where they were.

She called back the next morning, while Oona was looking at her suitcases, thinking she should start packing. The idea of it depressed her and she didn't want to leave. She wondered if the owners would let her stay for a few more weeks. She couldn't afford a very lengthy stay at the price she was paying. She thought the authorities would open the borders again in a few weeks. They couldn't keep the entire world shut down forever. No economy could afford it, although this was a situation that had never been seen before, since the Spanish flu, a century before.

"I have good news," the realtor said as soon as Oona answered the phone. The good news for Oona would be that she could stay a few weeks longer. The bad news would be having to pay for it, at the price she was paying now. "The owner is very sorry that you got stuck here. They're not locked down in Hong Kong yet, but the number of cases is increasing and they expect to be locked down soon too. They can't get into Europe now, even with their own plane, and they wouldn't come here anyway. They would probably go to their house in Gstaad, which is huge. In any case, they're very happy to let you stay as long as you want to. They have no other rentals on the books, and because this is really a force majeure event, they won't charge you rent. You're welcome to stay as their guest, until you can safely go back to the States." The realtor had been stunned by their offer, and so was Oona. They were lovely people.

"Oh my God, that's fantastic, and very generous of them. Please thank them for me. I'd be happy to pay something, if they'd prefer."

"Honestly, Mrs. Webster, they don't need the money. They hardly rent it out—I'm not sure why they even bother. The secretary said they like the idea of someone staying here. It keeps the staff working, if they're allowed to now, and if not, it keeps the house occupied. You've been a trouble-free tenant for the last month, and the secretary stressed that you're welcome to stay as long as you need to." It was the kindest thing anyone had done for her in years— they were just turning their home over to her and telling her to enjoy it.

She was suddenly a houseguest, not a tenant, which made her feel very special and spoiled. It made the decision easy. It wasn't going to cost her a penny, and she felt happy and comfortable in the house. As long as she was going to be in lockdown, better in France in the country than trapped in her empty, lonely apartment in New York. She had seen a video of New York on CNN, and it had looked like a ghost town. There wasn't a soul in the streets, the city was under total lockdown, and the ICU wards were overloaded. It didn't make returning to New York seem appealing or like a good idea. She called the head of her publishing division as soon as she hung up. She was a senior vice president whom Oona reported to, the rare times she had to, about a major corporate decision that needed their endorsement. Oona explained the situation and how dangerous it felt to travel home, and the senior VP agreed completely and told her to stay where she was. She could join any Zoom meetings she needed to, and she was easy to reach by email, or her American cell. The call was over in a minute, and Oona looked around with a grin when she hung up. Having been in France for a month, it already felt like home. She hadn't brought a lot of clothes with her, but she had what she needed, and she didn't need to dress up. She could just wear a nice sweater whenever she had to do FaceTime or Zoom. She was all set, and she walked up the stairs with a proprietary feeling. She suddenly felt that they had given her the house as a gift, and in fact they had. She made a mental note to buy them a very nice present when she left, probably something from Hermès. They had a lot of it in the house. She'd have to go to Paris for it when they were deconfined. And in the meantime she would be there, all by herself. The idea of it sounded great to Oona. She put on a heavy jacket, since it was chilly out, and went on a walk to celebrate her good fortune, thanking her lucky stars and the owners, who were letting her stay. It was the first time in a long time that someone, a stranger in this case, had been so kind to her.

She spoke to Marie on her way out, who had already received a text informing her that Oona was staying, and Oona asked her if she was comfortable working during the lockdown, and the housekeeper said she was. She agreed to come in for a half day every day, which was all Oona needed, to make her bed and clean the bathrooms and the kitchen. And as soon as the lockdown was lifted, she would go back to full-time, although Oona knew that she'd have to leave then and go back to New York. But half days were fine with her. She was all set.

She felt jubilant when she came back from her walk, knowing that La Belle Florence was hers for as long as she would be confined in France. And it hardly felt like a confinement in a place as beautiful as that, with gardens and forest land where she could walk freely.

She started her Zoom meetings three days later, which was supposed to be her first day back in the office. She began her workday at three P.M., which was nine A.M. in New York, and kept working and answering emails until eleven P.M., which was her normal eight-hour workday. She sent Gail an email to let her know what she'd done and got a response from her within minutes. "Welcome back," she wrote, joking with Oona.

The New York work schedule gave her the day free until three P.M. For her workday she wore a crisp white shirt, a nice sweater or one of the two jackets she had with her, and jeans, which no one could see on their screen, so she looked respectable on Face-Time or during Zoom meetings. It was how everyone else was working too, from their homes, and it was reasonably efficient, although not quite as much as being in the office, but it would work for as long as they'd have to do it, which Oona assumed wouldn't be for long. She couldn't imagine that the lockdown would last more than a few weeks. She had dinner during the New York lunch hour, seven P.M. for her. She propped her phone up on the counter in the kitchen, and several times had "lunch" on FaceTime with Gail, which was dinner for her. She gave her a tour around the house, and Gail was impressed by how beautiful it was.

"I'm not feeling sorry for you," Gail said ironically, "if that was the purpose of the tour." Oona had given her a glimpse of the grounds too, earlier in the day, and the first buds were beginning to appear in the garden, which would be a riot of color when they were in full bloom.

"It's lovely, isn't it?" Oona said, smiling. She felt almost proprietary about it.

"No, it's better than that. It's fabulous. I'd be jealous if I didn't like you so much." Gail grinned. "Where's Charles now, by the way? Is he back yet?"

"No," Oona said, "he's still in Argentina, taking tango lessons probably. I haven't told him that I stayed. I haven't heard from him since the kids left," and she didn't want to. "The kids are both fine about my staying here. They wanted me to. It's safer than New York." She wondered how Charles was experiencing Covid in Argentina but didn't want to contact him and ask.

"Where you are is a hell of a lot prettier than New York. Have you met any of your neighbors yet?" Gail asked, and Oona shook her head. The property was too big to have neighbors, and the only people she had seen locally were the people who ran the grocery store, the cheese shop, the wine shop, and the bookshop before it closed. The only thing you could buy during the lockdown was food, or anything sold at the pharmacy. The woman who ran the grocery store was chatty and spoke English, but no one else did. She loved gossiping about the locals and said there was an American at the château now too, but she never saw him. The employees at the château bought his groceries.

Oona was thinking of taking French lessons during her free hours before she started work every day. As her office, she was using a small study that looked a little like Madame de Pompadour's boudoir, and she switched to a library lined with antique books, which looked more businesslike and appropriate for a publisher of her stature, for her video meetings.

Oona was enjoying the time there more than ever, and as April approached, the weather was getting slightly warmer. Some mornings she painted with paints she had ordered online, or she sat in the sunshine and read. It was an extremely comfortable life. In April the weather warmed up considerably, and she looked healthy and relaxed during her Zoom meetings. Several people asked where she was, and she said she was in the country, and didn't tell them she was in France, in a fabulous house. They wouldn't have taken her seriously if she had, or they would have been jealous and nasty to her. Discretion seemed wiser.

She finally had an email from Charles in mid-April, six weeks after the kids had left, and a month after the lockdown began. He called her on FaceTime, which she didn't answer, and she returned the call on a normal line. She had no desire to show him the house that he had missed out on because he left her for Roberto. She didn't want the intimacy of seeing his face, or having him see hers. A normal phone call was enough.

"Where are you?" he asked her when she called him back. "I've been calling you everywhere, at the apartment, at your office, on your cell, in the Hamptons."

"I must have been on another line when you called. I'm working from home," she said. "The office is closed."

"Yours and everyone else's. The agency is closed too. I think a couple of diehards are still going in, but not many. Everyone is working remotely."

"We are too," she confirmed. "I'm actually working on our Christmas offerings now, to put in the catalogue. I'm hoping to get some of our authors on the *Times* list, and trying to figure out our strongest authors against the holiday competition." Her books weren't obvious holiday gifts since they were so literary, and had such a small, elite following.

"I know," he said quietly. It was like talking to a stranger now. She felt awkward with him, and she wondered what was happening in his life and didn't want to ask. "Are you in New York or the Hamptons?"

She hesitated before she answered. "I'm still in France. I didn't leave. I can work from here. Everyone else is remote, so I decided to stay."

"That must be costing you a fortune," he said, surprised.

"Actually not. The owners consider the confinement force majeure and are letting me stay here for free. They're really nice people." There was a long silence then, and for a minute she thought they'd been disconnected, and then he spoke in a nostalgic tone.

"I miss you, Oona." He sounded serious and a little bit lost.

"Everything okay in B.A.?" She tried to sound impersonal, not wanting to get in a long maudlin conversation with him about what had gone wrong in their marriage. She wondered if he was happy with Roberto, but she didn't want to know the answer. He had chosen a path, and he was on it. She had her life to live now, and he had his. "Have you talked to the kids?" she asked him. He was quiet for a few seconds before he answered.

"I emailed Will a few days ago, he hasn't answered. He must be busy." That or still angry at his father. "I heard from Meghan. She loves her job, and Africa."

"I know."

"How is Paris?" he asked her.

"I don't know. I haven't been to the city since the lockdown. I hear everything is shut down." They had been in lockdown for a month, and it had been extended for another month, with no sign of anything opening, but the days passed quickly. She was often surprised by how much so. With her work schedule, and a walk or some personal time before that, the days were flying by. She had been in France for two months, and there was no sign of anything changing. The prime minister spoke every two weeks to give them an update. The number of new cases had come down, but the hospitals were still jammed and there was no talk of deconfinement yet.

It was autumn in Argentina, and Charles had been there for nearly four months. They quickly ran out of things to say, and Oona cut the call short. It made her uncomfortable talking to him. He was an outsider now, part of her history, but not the present. He said he'd call her again soon, and she hoped he wouldn't. She didn't want to talk to him. She intended to talk to a lawyer but hadn't yet. She was letting time pass—she was still in no hurry, and she and Charles were both out of the country. The only link they had now were their children, who were adults, so there wasn't much to talk about. They would have to talk finances eventually, and division of property. She'd been thinking about it lately, and dreading it, the painful conversation of who owned what and how to divide things up, and what to sell.

Other than that, there was a sameness to the days. It was like *Groundhog Day*. Every day was a repeat of the last one, and she had settled into a routine over the last month, and the borders were showing no sign of opening.

There was talk of deconfinement but nothing concrete yet. Oona had heard from Gail that they were starting to let people go at Hargrove, replacing some of them with their counterparts at S&B, which had been expected, but since Oona and Gail weren't in the office to see the new faces appear and the disappearance of old ones, they weren't as aware of it as they would have been otherwise. Oona had noticed some new faces at Zoom meetings, but she was never sure if they were replacements or additions. She was counting on Gail for the gossip, but she didn't know either. Not going to the office made everyone feel disconnected.

On May first, when she went to the grocery store, Mme. Bertheaud, the owner, handed Oona a sprig of lily of the valley and explained that it was traditional on the first of May to give people a little stem of the delicate fragrant flower for good luck. Oona put it in a small vase when she got home. She liked the tradition. And the CEO of Hargrove, Martin Grass, called her right at the start of her workday and asked how she was holding up.

"Pretty well. I'm still in France," she told him. "There are worse places to be confined." He had called on a regular call, not Zoom or FaceTime, so she couldn't see him. They chatted for a few minutes about the extraordinary times in which they were living, and then he talked in circles about the changes that were happening as a result of the merger, and that were going to be happening in future. None of it sounded very exciting, and then he got to the point of why he had called her.

"We made a difficult decision as part of the rollout of our new plans after the merger," he explained. "It's not one I'm happy with, but it wasn't my decision. When you get this big, it's more about the bottom line, and the money boys call the shots. Publishing is changing, and the pandemic has put some heavy demands on us, to minimize our losses." Oona waited to hear the rest, and it took him a few minutes to get there. "We've always been very proud of your imprint, Oona. It's all about quality, not volume, but people aren't buying literary work right now. We have heavy competition from the streaming market, and people want shiny and new, they want easy to read, they don't want to be deeply intellectual during the pandemic. It's all about escape and distraction. We lose money on your imprint. We expect to. You don't publish work like that during hard times, though. During good times, we can afford it. But right now, with all the independent bookstores closed, I just can't justify it. I'm afraid we are going to shut the imprint down and turn the page. We need commercial fiction to compete with other publishers, not your list of literary authors. These are fast-moving times and we have to move fast with them."

"So you're transferring me to contemporary fiction?" she asked, sad to see the books she loved slip away into the past. She loved the books her imprint published and was proud of their authors.

"That was the hardest part of the decision," Martin said to her. "With the merger, we just have too many editors in commercial, contemporary fiction, and S&B has some really star editors in that category. We're bringing a number of them on board, which is bumping some of our people here out of their positions. It's a game of musical chairs now, and we just don't have seats for everyone. We're prepared to be generous with you, Oona—you made a niche for yourself that has worked for more than twenty years, but now it just doesn't, and I don't have a spot for you in contemporary, which is what's hot right now. Most of those editors are a lot younger and don't have your experience. With the imprint gone, it's not a fit with you anymore." As he said it, Oona understood what was happening.

"You're firing me?" Her voice was a squeak when she asked him.

"When this madness is over, I'm sure you will find something that works better for you at another house than anything we could offer you. I'm really sorry, Oona. We're going to miss you terribly. I wanted to let you know, in case you wanted to stay in France. You don't need to rush back now when the lockdown lifts." She mumbled a few banalities, and thanked him for letting her know. He told her she was getting a four-month severance, which wasn't overly generous, but aside from the money, which mattered to her, she was out of a job, and one that she had loved, effective immediately. Her imprint had published wonderful books, even though they had a small audience and weren't usually a commercial success. She felt terrible for her authors, who would now have a hard time getting published. But it was an antiquated arm of the business, a relic of the past, and so was she now. After twenty-five years with Hargrove, she'd just been fired. She felt foolish about starting to cry after they had hung up. He'd wished her the very best, and told her to be careful and stay healthy, all very trite.

Twenty-five years of love and devotion had ended, just like her marriage. Now out of a marriage and a job, she felt dazed as she sat at the desk in the little library. All she had left were her kids, no husband and no job. She was obsolete, washed up, finished, at forty-seven. Her whole professional identity had been that quality imprint, which was suddenly irrelevant and out of style. Hargrove was moving forward in a new direction, aggressively into the future with what people wanted now, and they wanted hot dogs and popcorn, not literary caviar or refinement. Martin Grass said there was a place for it in academic publishing, but not mainstream trade publishing. She felt almost as devastated as she had when Charles told her he was in love with Roberto. All the things that made up her identity were dissolving around her. She couldn't stop crying when she hung up.

She wanted to call Charles and tell him, as she would have in the past, but it was too humiliating. She had been fired. She felt totally irrelevant suddenly. She wanted to tell Gail, but she was too embarrassed, and afraid that they might be firing her too. In the current situation of no one in the office, her coworkers wouldn't see her leave the building or say goodbye. She would just vanish off their Zoom screens and be replaced by new people, and they would wonder what had happened to her. They would figure it out eventually but not quickly. She should have known when Martin called her. It was the death knell she hadn't understood at first, just as she had been shocked by Charles's announcement that he was leaving her for Roberto. She had no Roberto, no replacement for Charles standing by, and she didn't want one. Now she had no job.

She felt like a giant zero, and suddenly it felt like a double loss, a double failure on her part. No matter how nice or loyal or competent she had been, she couldn't hang on to a husband or a job. She felt as though she had nothing left except an apartment in New York and a house in the Hamptons, and she didn't even know who would own them after a divorce or if she and Charles would sell them. And she had two kids who were halfway around the world and would be ashamed of her for getting fired. Compounded with her separation, the loss of her job felt enormous, and how could she find a new job from here? She was overwhelmed by a feeling of loss and failure, and panic. Her world as she knew it lay in rubble at her feet.

As it turned out, the first of May wasn't her lucky day after all. She went upstairs to her bedroom and got into bed with her clothes on, and lay there until it got dark, feeling crushed. The spring sunshine was not for her, it was for people with husbands and jobs, who had purpose in their lives, and she had none. She had nothing to go home to, and no reason to go back to the States when they were deconfined. She felt as though her life was over. She didn't bother to eat. She lay in bed, mourning her life, until she finally fell asleep. She had no idea what she was going to tell her kids or anyone else, or when or how. When people asked what she did, all she could say was that she used to be an editor, and now she was nothing.

Chapter 5

Oona went out riding the day after she'd been fired, and for a long walk in the afternoon at the time when she was usually working. She was trying to clear her head. She felt dazed, as though she'd been in an accident and had a concussion. She went to bed without dinner again that night, which was her usual reaction to catastrophe or major stress. She couldn't eat.

In a moment of panic the following day, she called Nancy Green, a headhunter she knew in New York who specialized in publishing, and said she was thinking of making a change, and the headhunter was candid with her.

"We've had a lot of calls this week from Hargrove editors. There's a bloodbath happening there. They seem to be keeping the S and B editors and letting a lot of the Hargrove editors go." Oona finally admitted that she was one of them and that her imprint was being shut down.

"I'm sad to hear it," Nancy Green said. "I love that imprint. The problem is that it's not commercially viable. You need to get into commercial fiction to stay with the times. You're young enough to do that, Oona. It's kind of like being a Shakespearean actor. It's wonderful experience, but it's not where the world is today. When you come back to New York, you'll need to be ready to move on to the commercial world. It's an adjustment, and you've got time to get ready for it. No one is hiring right now. You need to ride out the pandemic and come back ready to jump into the shark tank with everyone else." It sounded hideous to Oona and like an apt description of what she had to look forward to. She got a headache thinking about it.

Her safe little world had been shattered, far from all the aggressive competition she would have to deal with now when she went back. But publishing was all she knew, and she had to grow with it. She dreaded going back now more than ever. It wasn't just about an empty apartment, it was about an empty life and no career. She felt like her life was over at forty-seven. Another twenty-five years wasted and down the tubes, while the parade of the employed marched past her and passed her by, just like Charles and Roberto. And she knew she had to say something to her children about getting fired.

It took her another week to do that, while she tried to heal from the blow she'd been dealt. She told Meghan in an email, and tried to sound upbeat, which she could do better in email than by phone. She called Will and told him. He was sympathetic and tried to bolster her spirits, and she let him think he had. But she was very down, and didn't want to speak to anyone. She was in deep mourning for her lost job.

She had four messages from Gail, which she hadn't answered yet. Clearly, she had heard the news, and Oona didn't feel ready to talk to her. She sent her a text and promised to call soon. Gail left her alone after that, until Oona reached out to her. Gail knew that Oona disappeared when times were bad, hiding deep in the forest until she felt ready to face the world again. This was a hard blow, and it had been a hard six months for her. But she was smart and talented, and Gail knew she would be fine. But Oona didn't know that yet. There was life after Hargrove Publishing, after Charles Webster, and after the pandemic. She just had to get there, and fight to rise from the ashes, which was easier said than done.

The long walks on the property helped, and so did driving through the countryside in the little battered car she had rented. She didn't want to see people or talk to anyone. She needed to be alone to digest what had happened. Her children were alive and healthy, and she knew Charles wouldn't let her starve. She had money saved and invested. Even Oona knew that her life wasn't as over as she feared, but it felt awful. All the yardsticks she had used to measure her success in life had been broken and thrown away. Her marriage and her job. She'd been downsized. She looked at herself in the mirror one morning and hated what she saw. She looked beaten. It had been a week since she had been fired. She told herself to get over it and get a life. No one had died. She didn't have a terminal illness. She didn't have Covid. And if she had to join the sharks in the pool of commercial fiction, so be it. She couldn't let getting fired devour her. She hadn't lost an arm or a leg. She had lost a job.

She drove into the village to buy groceries, took a different route home, and came across a lake she had never seen before. She got out and decided to walk around it, and when she had, she sat on the narrow rim of sand in the May sunshine and felt its warmth on her face, and could sense herself slowly coming back to life again. She lay back on the sand and looked up at the sky, and there were giant white balls of fluffy clouds in a cameo blue sky, and she could see them moving. She knew the clouds in her sky would move too, and she had to move with them. Maybe she'd find a better job, one she liked as much or more. She had been comfortable and complacent for years where she was, now she had to reach out and stretch and find something else. Somewhere in her misery, she had turned a corner. There had been enough loss in her life in the past six months, and now she had to get back on her feet again.

She stood up to leave and heard whimpering from a cluster of bushes nearby. She turned toward the sound, and thought she had imagined it, and then she heard it again. The sound was louder the second time. It sounded like a cat, or maybe a bird, some small animal in the bushes. She walked toward them and pushed the branches apart, hoping that some wild creature didn't jump out and bite her, and she found herself looking into a little white face with a round black nose, and sad eyes looking up at her as it whimpered again. It was a little dog with floppy ears and curly hair just long enough to get tangled up in the branches at the base, and it was held fast and couldn't free itself. She knelt down next to it, still holding the branches back. It was a small white dog covered in dirt with pleading eyes.

"How did you get yourself in this mess?" she asked the little face, and it whimpered again. She wished she had something to cut him loose with, but she didn't. She took her car keys out of her pocket, and worked on severing the tangles of fur that were caught in the branches and keeping the little dog prisoner. It took her nearly an hour and she finally freed the little dog, and it limped out of the bushes, and climbed into her lap as though to thank her. There were bald patches where it had fought to free itself, and Oona held it for a minute as it licked her face. She could see it was a female and she had an injured paw.

Oona stood looking at her. "Now what do we do?" she asked her. There was no way she could leave her there. She was injured, lost, and possibly abandoned, and probably hungry. She was panting and probably thirsty too. There was no way of knowing how long she'd been trapped in the bushes. Oona picked her up and walked to the car, as the little ball of tangled fluff wagged her tail and barked at her. Oona smiled. "You're welcome. You can come home with me for now, and maybe we can find your owner." She laid the little dog down on the passenger seat, and as soon as she got into the car the little dog climbed into Oona's lap and lay there until they got to the house, and then Oona carried her inside. Marie had already left for the day. Oona took her into the kitchen, and set down a bowl of water for her, and she drank half of it, while Oona cut up little bits of chicken from her dinner the night before and set it down in another bowl. The little dog was ravenous and ate it all, and wagged her tail at Oona when she finished. She was small and a mixture of some kind, and she was filthy and looked pathetic with her bald patches where her fur had been torn away by the branches as she must have fought to free herself.

Oona filled the sink with warm water, gently put her in it, and carefully examined the paw. She had a cut on it, but it didn't look too deep, and Oona discovered as she washed her that she was snow-white when she was clean. She rinsed her and dried her with a towel, and set her back down on the floor, where the little dog finished the water and limped around the kitchen wagging her tail. Oona carried her out to the garden so she could do what she needed to, and she seemed very well behaved, and then Oona carried her back into the house. She wanted to take her to a vet to see if she had a chip with an owner's address. She was very sweet and wasn't afraid of Oona, so she guessed she must have been well treated by her owners. She was probably someone's beloved pet. Oona had no idea where to find a vet until Marie came back the next day and could tell her, and the little dog followed her out of the kitchen and into the study where she'd been working every day until she lost her job. She told herself that the last thing she needed now was a dog, but she had no idea what to do with her, and she would have to keep her until she could take her to the vet the next day and maybe someone had been looking for her and would claim her. "Just for tonight," she said to her, and the dog wagged her tail as though she agreed. She tilted her head when Oona talked to her, and she was adorable.

Oona carried her upstairs to her bedroom, and the little ball of patchy white fur jumped into a comfortable chair, curled up and went to sleep, as Oona smiled at her. She had a feeling that the dog was an omen of some kind, but she wasn't sure of what. New beginnings, maybe, or recovery, or healing, or just the dose of love that they both needed, for a night anyway. She didn't intend to keep her and hoped to find her owner.

She fed her again at dinnertime, and the dog ate everything. Oona took her outside and she did what she was supposed to do again. She appeared to be housebroken, and Oona made a bed for her of a soft blanket that was lying on a chair in her bedroom and the dog curled up in it, after licking Oona's hand, and went to sleep, and slept soundly until morning, when Oona took her downstairs to the kitchen to feed her, then outside. When Marie saw the dog, she made a fuss over her. Oona explained to her that she needed to find a vet, and Marie wrote down the name of one nearby, just beyond the villages, and drew a little map of how to get there. Oona took the dog there after breakfast.

Miraculously, the vet spoke enough English that Oona could explain to him how she had found her, and she showed him the cut on her paw. He bandaged her and checked her and said she was about a year old. She had no microchip, but she had been neutered, and she was definitely housebroken and had made no mistakes. She was clearly someone's pet that had gotten lost or had been abandoned, and without a chip or a collar with tags on it, there was no way to find the owner.

"You've never seen her before?" Oona asked him and he shook his head. And there were no photos of lost dogs in his waiting room that looked like her.

"Some people come from far away to that lake," he said. "Perhaps they forgot her, or she was trapped in the bush and they couldn't find her when they go away. I think she is yours now. She loves you," he said, smiling, as the little ball of white fluff with the black button nose licked his hand.

"I'm here for the confinement, but I'm going back to New York," she said.

"You will need a shot for the *rage,* to go to America with her."

"Rabies?" Oona asked, not sure about *rage,* and guessing, and he laughed.

"Yes. I give her a shot now, and a paper you can show." He gave the dog a shot, and then handed her back to her new owner. Oona still wasn't sure what to do with her, but she'd had her shot now, and he gave her a chip before they left, and used his address to identify her if she got lost again. Oona wondered if Marie would want her. She wanted to find her a home before she left. She was such a loving little dog, she deserved a good home, and she was clean and white now. But Oona couldn't see herself taking a dog back to New York.

They were back at the house an hour later and Oona asked Marie if she wanted to keep her. She had no known owner. Marie said she had two big dogs at home and couldn't take her. Oona sat in the chair in the library, stroking her, and she fell asleep as Oona thought of a name for her. The name of the mistress for whom the house had been built. Florence. Flo. Oona set her gently down in the chair, and Florence lay there snoring softly, as Oona put all her work papers in a stack to send back to Hargrove. She was going to send them to Gail to return them, since the office was closed.

It was the end of a chapter in her life. It had been six months of chapter endings, and it was time for new beginnings. Maybe Florence was a sign of those new beginnings. If so, she had made a ragtag entry into Oona's life, filthy, injured, bedraggled, abandoned, but ready for a new life and to start over. Maybe she was a sign after all. All she wanted was to follow Oona around and love her, and maybe she was just what Oona needed, someone to love and to love her. There were worse fates for a curly-haired little white dog. She had gotten lucky when Oona heard her and saved her. Her fur would grow back and her paw would heal, just like Oona's wounded heart. Maybe it wasn't an accident that she had found her, Oona wondered, perhaps it was meant to be, and Florence was an omen of good things to come, for both of them. Florence seemed pleased with the arrangement as she lay on her back with all four paws in the air, snoring softly.

After a week of mourning her lost job, three days after Oona had found Florence trapped in the bushes, the President declared France deconfined. Freedom! The outer borders of Schengen Europe remained closed to outsiders, but all the countries within those borders, and France in particular, were open to each other again. The Schengen borders were like an invisible boundary that encircled all the countries in Europe. People could cross from one European country freely into another, but the outer borders required a passport to enter or exit Europe. So for the moment, foreigners like Americans outside the borders could not enter Europe, but anyone in Europe could travel from one European country to another.

After two months of lockdown, stores could open, people could return to work, children could go back to school, businesses could function, and restaurants with outdoor terraces followed rapidly. Deconfinement had come in two months. There was a feeling of celebration, and people's moods lifted. It reminded Oona of scenes of the liberation of Paris during World War II, in photos she had seen. People were happy and felt alive again. It was mid-May, and the countryside was in full bloom, as were the gardens of La Belle Florence, which were even prettier than Oona could have guessed in February.

Oona called the car service a few days later and was driven to Paris to go shopping and enjoy the bustle of the city. People smiled at each other in the street, some wearing masks, not all. For months, they had been told they didn't need them, and now they did. But not everyone followed the new rule.

She had lunch at an outdoor café and sat basking in the sun at the end of the meal. She even went to a dog shop and bought a collar and leash for Florence and some toys and sweaters, and two beds, for her bedroom and the kitchen. She had left Florence at home with Marie. She came back at seven o'clock that night, with the car full of shopping bags from her forays in Paris. And she had even bought a big straw hat to wear in the garden. Florence loved her toys when Oona put them on the floor for her. She didn't mind the pink collar Oona had bought her, though she was less enchanted with the sweaters, which fit perfectly. Her fur had already started to grow back. Oona had had a wonderful day in Paris. On the way home, she was thinking about when she should leave. But by then the United States was not doing as well as France, and it still seemed unsafe to return to New York, and she had no reason to go back now. No kids, no man, no job. There didn't seem to be much point to it, and La Belle Florence had never looked better in all its early summer glory with vivid colored flowers in the garden. It seemed like the right place to be for now.

Two days later, she was buying groceries at Mme. Bertheaud's and had a car full of food and other purchases to take home, when she decided to stop for coffee at a café in the village. It was so exciting to see people again, and everything in motion. Oona loved it and couldn't get enough of it. Even the sleepy village of Milly-la-Forêt had come alive again, and everyone was in a good mood. There was the illusion that Covid was over, which was not the case, but the number of new daily cases was low enough to make it possible to end the lockdown for now, unless it got worse again.

She sat down at a table partially shaded by an umbrella, turned her face to the sun after her first sip of coffee, and heard a mellifluous voice of a man chatting to the waitress behind her. She recognized it as an accent from somewhere in the Caribbean, although she wasn't sure precisely where. She glanced over at them talking, and the man looked vaguely familiar, but she couldn't place him. She had the distinct impression that she had seen him somewhere, and he would have been difficult to forget. He had dark shining skin, a brilliant smile of perfect white teeth, expressive dark eyes, and his hair was done in what looked like corks standing out all over his head. The hairstyle suited him, and he looked animated and laughed as he talked to the waitress in fluent French. He was tall and powerfully built. He was a strikingly beautiful man one wouldn't soon forget, and it was a pleasure just looking at him.

Oona finished her coffee, and the waitress managed to tear herself away to give Oona her check. The man with the Caribbean accent was wearing a crisp snow-white shirt with a stand-up collar and perfectly pressed jeans, as he glanced at Oona and cast his dazzling smile at her. He had laughter in his eyes and spoke to her in English from where he was sitting.

"I'm sorry to be rude, but I can't help but ask, are you the American who's living at La Belle Florence?" he asked her, and she nodded with a shy smile. He had a way of commanding one's attention without trying to. He was easy to talk to, with a warm, engaging manner, and a deep, almost musical voice. There was something oddly familiar about his voice, as though she'd heard it before.

"I am," she admitted.

"I've read so much about that house and the woman who inspired it. I'm in love with it. Is it as beautiful as they say?" he asked her. "I've even studied drawings of it and the original plans. I am fascinated by a woman who inspired so much love that someone built it for her, with care for every detail. The flowers in the moldings on the walls are of her favorite flowers," he told her.

"Are you an architect?"

He smiled his breathtaking smile at the question and shook his head. He looked easygoing, at ease, and exuded an air of happiness.

"No, I just love old houses. I'm staying at the Château Bertigny for a year. I was planning to use it as a base, and I just spent two months in lockdown there. It's nice to be out again, isn't it?" he said. He was at the café for the same reason Oona was, the sheer joy of seeing people again.

98

Oona smiled back at him. "Mme. Bertheaud in the grocery store told me an American was living there. You don't sound American." She laughed.

"I'm not. I'm from Tobago, a small island off Trinidad—that's where my family lives now, in Port of Spain, the capital. And you?"

"New York."

"There's nowhere like Tobago," he said proudly. "If you speak English here, they think you're American—they can't discern the difference in our accents. I live in L.A. though, and London before that." She could hear just a touch of British in his Island accent, which was quite pronounced, despite Mme. Bertheaud's interpretation of it as American. He continued to look familiar to Oona, and she still had no idea where she'd seen him, after talking to him. Or maybe he just seemed familiar because he was so friendly.

"If it wouldn't be too inconvenient, I would love to see La Belle Florence one day. I've studied every detail of it. I hope the owners haven't spoiled it. I wonder if the tunnels and secret passages that led to the old château before it burned are still there."

"I don't know." She smiled as she stood up. "I wouldn't want to get stuck in them if they are. But you're welcome to come out and take a look whenever you want."

"Thank you, I'd love that," he said warmly but politely. He wasn't fresh or overly familiar. "I'll take you up on it if you don't mind. Would tomorrow work for you?" he asked her. "I can do it another day if you prefer." He was quick to accept her offer.

"Tomorrow is fine." Now that she wasn't working, she had nothing on her calendar, no Zoom meetings or conference calls. No FaceTime or Skype. She was painting in her free time. And he seemed to have spare time too. They had all lived with nothing but time for the past two months in the isolation of confinement. "I'll see you tomorrow then," she said shyly. Neither of them had volunteered their names. They left the café at the same time, and he got on his bicycle while she got into her car. He was even taller than she had guessed when he was sitting, with broad shoulders, a small waist, and long legs. He waved as he took off at a good speed. He was a beautiful man, and she was still thinking of him when she suddenly realized who he was as she drove home. It hit her like a lightning bolt and she laughed out loud. She felt like an idiot. But she hadn't expected to meet him in the little village in France.

"Oh my God," she said, laughing at herself. She had no idea why she hadn't recognized him, since he always wore his hair in the same unusual style. He was Ashley Rowe, a famous actor, one of the biggest in Hollywood. She couldn't wait to tell Meghan she had met him. All Oona could remember was that he had come from England after starring in a hit police series, and had been making major movies and series in L.A. ever since. She just hadn't expected to see him in Milly-la-Forêt. She could envision him easily at the château where he was staying. It was the one that Mme. Bertheaud said belonged to the big British movie producer, who never used it anymore and lent it to friends, which made total sense now that she knew who he was.

Florence was waiting for Oona when she got home and was thrilled to see her. She did a little dance around Oona. She took her out to play in the garden, where she chased squirrels and birds, and enjoyed it thoroughly. She dashed into the flower beds, and

Oona scolded her and took her out, and she looked up at Oona adoringly.

Oona wondered if Ashley Rowe would come the next day or if he would forget and have something better to do. It seemed incredible that in that small, quiet village, she had met a major movie star, and there was no one but Florence to tell about it. She could hardly wait to tell Meghan the next time she called.

Chapter 6

Oona was in the garden playing with Flo when Ashley Rowe suddenly appeared at ten-thirty the next morning. He had bicycled from the Château Bertigny and looked hesitant when he saw Oona and the dog running down a path with one of Flo's new toys. Oona was throwing it for her.

"I'm sorry. Is it too early? I'm an early riser and I don't have your number. I thought I'd drop by to see if you were around, on my way to the village."

"I'm up early too," she said, smiling at him, less at ease with him than she had been the day before now that she had realized who he was. He was wearing black jeans and a black sweater and running shoes, with his hair in his familiar style.

"The gardens are spectacular," he said, admiring them, and then crouched down to pet the dog. She still looked a little moth-eaten, with the bald spots inflicted by the bush where she'd been trapped, but there was already a light fuzz over them, and her face was so sweet, she was impossible to resist. She wagged her tail and barked at him and brought her toy over for him to throw. He obliged her and tossed it a few feet away and she dashed back with it for him to throw again. He stood up and smiled at Oona. "She's adorable. Is she a puppy?" Florence was dancing around him trying to get him to throw her toy again, and he did.

"The vet says she's about a year old. I just found her recently, tangled up in a bush at a lake not far from here. I rescued her, and she seems to have moved in."

"You could do a lot worse," he said, and she laughed. "I have occasionally. Will you take her home with you when you go back? I assume you're going back," he said. He stood very tall beside her, and had the body of an athlete. He was an amazing-looking man, and Oona was trying not to be too visibly in awe of him. He looked every inch like the star he was. He was totally at ease and self-confident as he smiled at Oona. He wasn't arrogant, just comfortable, and totally natural chatting with her about the dog, as though they were old friends.

"Yes, I am going back to New York," she answered his question. "I don't know when. I'm in no hurry. One of my children is in Kenya, working at a children's refugee center, and my son is in San Francisco, with Google. And I've been working remotely, but I'm done with that now, and after two months of confinement, I figure I might as well enjoy it while I'm here. France seems to be safer than New York at the moment, so here I am."

"That's how I feel," he said seriously. "L.A. is out of control. We're better off in France. It's not a hardship being here." He smiled at her. He wasn't seductive, he was friendly and warm and open, and he had a dazzling smile.

"I rented the house for a month in February, and I'm still here three months later. My landlords have been very kind about it. I think they own the house out of sentiment, but apparently it's too small for them. They're a big Hong Kong family, and they rent it out occasionally, so I'm the lucky winner on this one," Oona explained.

"I feel that way too," he said, as they strolled slowly toward the house and Florence followed, carrying her little toy in her mouth, waiting to drop it at his feet again. "An English friend I worked with rented me the château for a year, for a dollar." He grinned, his gorgeous smile lighting up his face, and she noticed that his eyes seemed to dance when he laughed. He looked like a happy person and had an upbeat energy about him that was contagious. "I got the best end of that deal too. He doesn't come here anymore. I came over from L.A. the day before they locked down and the borders closed. I figured it was providence and I was meant to be here." He looked peaceful as he said it, as they stopped outside the main entrance to the house. It was an enormous eighteenth-century shiny black door with a brass knocker.

"I was on vacation when the recall came to go back to the States, so I stayed. Do you want to come in?" she asked him, and he beamed again.

"I'm dying to. I feel as though I've been here before, I've looked at the photographs of it so often. When I rented Bertigny, I researched the historical buildings and homes in the area, and I read about this one. La Belle Florence has the most romantic history, and perhaps the most tragic one. Florence de Montmarrin was sixteen when she became the king's mistress. Her father was a viscount and turned a blind eye to the king's passionate love for his daughter. She lived at the palace as part of his court, and he built this house for her when she was seventeen. He spent a great deal of time here with her. His country château was a short walk away, and they had underground passageways to connect them so he could visit her easily and safely." They were standing in the front hall when he told her the story in hushed tones, and she listened raptly. He made the young girl's story come alive with his deep smooth voice, and his lilting Caribbean accent, which made it sound even more picturesque. Oona knew the story, but he made Florence seem even more real to her. She could almost imagine her standing in the hall with them.

"When Florence was twenty, the king took another mistress, a much older married woman, a duchess, who outranked Florence. He had been with Florence for quite a long time by then, four years, which in those days was an eternity, given how short their life spans were," he said, and Oona nodded. "According to what I read about it, he spent time with both women then, but Florence was his true love. They say she had the face of an angel, and laughed and smiled all the time, and delighted him. Apparently, the duchess was a fiercely jealous woman, and Florence died in her sleep in her rooms at the palace. The king found her himself and was inconsolable. It was believed that she was poisoned. She was twenty-one years old. The king was certain that the duchess had done it. He banished her from court immediately and sent her back to her husband, somewhere in the provinces. She never returned to court. He kept the house as it had been when Florence was alive, as a sort of shrine to her and how much he loved her. He came here to the house often by himself. It saved his life—he was here the night the rebels burned his château to the ground near here, and he hid in one of the underground passages. The rebels never touched this house. It remained as perfect as it had been when Florence was alive. She died in 1787, two years before the Revolution. He died in 1793, six years after she did. He was executed. The locals believed that her ghost was here after she died, because she'd been happy here and loved the house. Perhaps because the king was often here then, the house still seemed inhabited after she died. According to the history, she was his last mistress until his death in the Revolution. He was the last king, and she was his last love. It's a beautiful story, isn't it? This is the charming refuge and love nest he built for her," Ashley said, smiling at Oona. "It makes me happy, and I feel close to them just being here. She was a beautiful blond girl, very small and delicate, barely bigger than a child, and she was so young. It was a great honor when he took her as his mistress. All the women in the court were jealous, particularly when he built her a country house. She wanted it to be very simple and rural, with lovely gardens, and that's what he gave her. The gardens still look very similar to the way they did then. He had his own gardeners and arborists design them, and they look almost the same, from some watercolors I've seen. I think Florence may have done the paintings herself. I can see why your landlords are sentimental about this house," he said nostalgically, glancing around, and he pointed to a detail in the ceiling which Oona hadn't noticed before, little angels amid garlands of flowers as part of the relief work. She walked him into the living room and he stood admiring everything, and the way it was furnished with eighteenth-century antiques.

"I think it's grander than it was then," Ashley said, and followed her into the dining room, and the library she had used as an office for the first two months.

He moved closer to the books and examined them closely and then turned to Oona. "May I touch the books?" he asked her respectfully, and she nodded, as he removed two books from one shelf and four from the one below it, setting them carefully on the table she had used as a desk. He reached into the bookcase and pressed a lever, and suddenly an entire panel of books sprang open farther down the wall, revealing a hiding place beyond it. It was dusty, and they could see a door that had been sealed over. Oona's eyes were wide as she examined it with him. "There are a number of panels like this in the house, so she could hide if she needed to, or maybe he just designed it for fun. I'll have to give you the book about them. There's a lot in it about the house. I fell in love with them after I read it. I'm not sure how lovable he was, but she sounded enchanting, like a little elf, and she was very mischievous, which he loved." Ashley had brought the house even more alive for Oona, and they went upstairs after that, and found another secret panel in her dressing room. The little dog backed away when they opened it, and like the other one it had been sealed closed, perhaps by more recent or even the current owners. "That one led to a staircase, I think, that leads to the basement," Ashley explained.

They finished the tour of the house, and Oona made him a cup of coffee, and they sat down at the kitchen table. It was Saturday and Marie was off, so they were alone. After spending almost two hours together, Oona felt at ease with him. There was nothing showy about him, nor anything to suggest that he was a star. She knew who he was now, and she had forgotten to tell him her name, and he hadn't asked.

"That was fascinating, thank you." She gazed at him.

"I've been dying to come and see the house since I got here. Bertigny isn't nearly as interesting. It's very serious and straightforward, with beautiful details, but nothing as much fun as this or with as much soul. I'll give you the book about La Belle Florence the next time I see you."

"Have you been to any of the local *brocantes* yet?" she asked him, since he seemed to enjoy history.

"I have." He smiled at her. "And all the antique shops between here and Paris, and a couple of auctions. I collect fascinating old objects. I've got several things I want to take home."

"Me too," she admitted.

"There's a good one every Saturday about twenty miles from here, near a farmer's market. I want to go next weekend. I think things may be a little slower right now. I also want to go to the Hôtel Drouot in Paris. I love their auctions. I'll call and see if they're open." When they finished their coffee, he put his cup in the sink and they walked outside. The gardeners were busy. Ashley and Oona had spent a lovely morning together, which had turned out to be a history lesson for her. She loved the house even more now.

"There's a beautiful little chapel near here if you haven't been there yet, if you like old churches. Saint-Blaise des Simples—it's twelfth-century and Jean Cocteau is buried there."

"I do love old churches," she said. He acted as though they were going to see each other again, as they walked to where he had leaned his bicycle against a tree. She was still a little awestruck that she had just spent almost two hours with Ashley Rowe, talking as though they were old friends.

"Do you like Cajun food?" he asked her, and she smiled.

"I do."

"You'll have to come to dinner at the house. I love to cook. I've been trying new recipes during the confinement. I had my mother send me my favorite ones, and she showed me how to do them on Skype. Everyone in my family loves to cook."

"Do you have a big family?" she asked, curious about him. He seemed so happy and comfortable in his own skin, with no airs and graces, which made her curious about how he grew up.

"There are seven of us. I'm the only one who left the islands. The others are still there. I try to get home a few times a year. I'm the oldest, and my youngest sister is sixteen. My father works for the post office in Port of Spain now, and my mother is a teacher, or was—she just retired. My father is still working. We were poor but happy. We lived in Tobago then, and now they live in Trinidad, in the capital. I missed Tobago, so I bought a house there a few years ago. I try to go back as often as I can, but it's never enough. My parents saved to send me to the Royal Academy of Dramatic Arts in London when I was eighteen. I was a Shakespearean actor in London before I got a part in a series, and then went to Hollywood. I've been there for seven years now. It's a very different life," he said. He looked nostalgic when he spoke of Trinidad and To- bago. He was by no means the American the locals thought he was, far from it. If anything, he was more British, and seemed more European than American. "The house we lived in, in Tobago, didn't even have electricity when I was growing up. It sounds crazy, but I miss that sometimes. It was so simple and happy." He swung onto his bicycle then. It had been an amazing morning with him, and the time had flown. He was wonderful to talk to, and they were both starving for conversation with other humans, and social contact after the lockdown. "I'll let you know when I'm going to a *brocante*—maybe you'd like to come with me," he said, and looked hesitant. She didn't have the feeling that he was flirt- ing with her, he was just congenial. And then he laughed. "I've been very rude. I was so excited to see the house, I forgot to intro- duce myself." He was used to people knowing who he was. "Ashley Rowe," he said, and smiled at her.

"Oona Kelly," she said, dropping Charles's last name, which she had wanted to do for months, and this seemed like a good time. He rode down the driveway on his bike, and turned to wave at her, and she felt as though she had a new friend, a fascinating one. She had never met anyone like him, and she hoped she'd see him again. He had a joie de vivre and a natural simplicity without arti- fice or pretension, and a thirst for knowledge and connection with people. They exchanged phone numbers, and she hoped he would drop by again.

She went back into the house with her new information about its history and secrets, which endeared the place to her even more, and Florence followed her inside. Oona felt a little guilty now for naming the dog after the king's lovely ill-fated young mistress. She made a salad for lunch, with lettuce fresh from the vegetable garden, and tomatoes grown there too, and she realized again how lucky she was to be there, instead of lonely in her apartment in New York. She wouldn't have met Ashley Rowe if she was in New York. She would think of his visit that morning and all she had learned about him when she saw his movies now. He was a wonderful actor, with depth to his performances, and now she knew how well trained he was, and why he was such a great actor. There was a "realness" to him. He was a whole person, with an interesting history, a real life, and a family he was close to.

She went to the village herself that afternoon, to buy a chicken for dinner, and more cheese at the cheese shop. She wondered when she'd see Ashley again and if he'd really invite her to a meal he cooked himself. He was very down-to-earth, which made him appealing and genuine. She knew he was younger than she was, but she couldn't remember exactly how old he was, and looked him up on Google when she got back to the house. He was thirty-nine years old, but he looked even younger, and she read that he was divorced and had two children, a son and a daughter, and that his English ex-wife was an actress who had also attended the Royal Academy of Dramatic Arts, so Oona guessed they must have met at school. They had been married for seven years and divorced for six. There were photos of him with various famous actresses. He had won a Golden Globe award, and had been nominated for an Oscar, but hadn't won. He'd had a very impressive career so far. Oona recognized all the women he had dated. They were all stars.

And though his beautiful ex-wife wasn't as big a star as he was, she looked familiar to Oona.

Oona was watching a movie on her computer when Meghan called her that night. She was at a village near the refugee camp to buy supplies, where she could get cell phone service, so she called her mother. It was a nice surprise for Oona, and Meghan told her all the news from the camp. The incidence of Covid was still very low in the area and she felt safe there. Then Oona teased her with her own news.

"You'll never guess who I met in the village yesterday. He's living here, at the château. I didn't recognize him at first." Meghan went down a list of possible subjects, and finally ran out of names.

"Ashley Rowe," Oona said nonchalantly, as though meeting him was a common occurrence. Meghan let out a scream, vastly impressed.

"Did you talk to him?" Meghan was curious about him. He was a very handsome, impeccably groomed man, and a great actor with charisma and a style all his own.

"Yes, he came to the house and knew the whole history. He even showed me some secret panels that probably lead to the tunnels that are sealed off."

"I'm a huge fan. Is he nice? I think he's from Jamaica or something."

"Trinidad, or Tobago more exactly," her mother said knowledgably.

"I wish I'd been there. I've seen all his movies and watched the series he was in. He's a huge deal, Mom."

"I know."

"Do you think you'll see him again?"

"I don't know. Maybe. He said he'd invite me to the château for a home-cooked meal." It was what she loved about being deconfined now—you could see people, talk to them, meet new ones, go to stores and go wherever you wanted. The two-month lockdown had seemed endless and was a severe deprivation of human contact. She was in an extremely comfortable situation, but had no one to talk to.

"You have to go if he invites you, Mom. Promise me. I'd love to meet him one day."

"I don't know if he'll call me or see me again. I'm sure he has better things to do than hang out with me."

"Would you date him?" Meghan was curious. The subject of her mother dating hadn't come up so far, but sooner or later it would. Oona was still a beautiful woman, only in her forties, and had a long life ahead of her. She wasn't going to spend it alone. But she didn't want to think about it now. She wasn't ready.

"No, of course not, he's eight years younger than I am. That's way too much to date. I'd feel ridiculous, and I don't want to date anyone for now. I'm married to your father," she said firmly. She was still getting over the blow Charles had dealt her and wasn't sure what the future held. "Besides, he wasn't trying to pick me up. It was just friendly. You can tell he likes people. He's full of life."

"I can't believe you met him." Meghan was in awe of her mother's new friend. "And you're free to do whatever you want, Mom, given what Dad is doing in Buenos Aires. Maybe you'll meet someone nice in France." She didn't approve of the way her father had treated her mother, running off with someone else, whether male or female. Oona never talked to her children about it and didn't want to create a wedge between them and their father, but Meghan knew that she was deeply hurt, and both she and Will were totally sympathetic to her and angry at their father. And now she was alone in France in the pandemic while he played in Buenos Aires. It seemed completely irresponsible and unkind to Meghan, and selfish of him. She had seen her father in a new very unflattering light. "You should call Ashley Rowe and invite him to dinner, Mom. Don't wait for him to call you. Maybe he's shy. And he's probably lonely too. All my friends I hear from are isolated and sound depressed." The situation was depressing worldwide. Oona smiled at her daughter's aspirations for her and was touched.

"He doesn't look lonely or depressed, and I don't want him to think I'm chasing him. Women must pursue him all the time." It was obvious from his striking good looks. And she had gotten no sexual or courting vibe from him, which was a relief. She wasn't open to it, and didn't want to think about it, which made Ashley Rowe even more appealing as a friend, because nothing romantic would ever happen between them. Their difference in age, history, and lifestyle made her ineligible, even if she wanted a romance with him, which she didn't. Race didn't enter into it, it was irrelevant. And no matter how unassuming he was, he was a huge star and she was a mere mortal. She wasn't narcissistic enough, or at all, to think he was attracted to her. He could date any woman he wanted, and had dated many famous women. And she was an unemployed book editor, she was no one at all compared to him.

* * *

As it turned out, Ashley didn't call her, and Oona didn't call him either. She didn't need to. She ran into him at the cheese store in town. He looked surprised and happy to see her. It had been a week since they'd met, everything was in full bloom, and the weather was balmy. He smiled as soon as he saw her.

"Do you want to go to a *brocante* with me tomorrow?" he asked her after they chatted for a few minutes.

"I'd love it," she said easily. Her eyes and face came to life when she saw him. He was the only person she knew in France.

"I'm sorry I didn't come by last week. My agent sent me a script after I saw you, and I've been studying it and making notes, trying to figure out if I want to do it. I was supposed to be working on a new series right now. It got postponed because of Covid, and it looks like it will fall apart and get canceled. The female lead and the director are sick, and the investors are getting cold feet. The one I've been reading might be a good replacement for it. I have a shot at a part in a British series too, and I'm trying to figure out if I want to be in L.A. or here in Europe. It's a nice problem to have, a choice of projects, with so many people out of work." He smiled sheepishly. "Acting is a weird business. One day you're on top, and the next day, you can be out on your ear and it's all over. I try to remember that. Nothing is sure in this business." But he was so well established now, and so talented, that Oona couldn't imagine him being out of favor. He was too famous to be forgotten, and was in high demand, but he seemed very modest about it.

They chatted for a few minutes and then went their separate ways. She had a long list of emails to answer that she hadn't been in the mood to deal with before, including an inquiry from a real estate broker about renting the house in the Hamptons since it was standing empty, but if she went home before the summer she'd want to use it, and Charles said the same when she asked him via email. He said that if Roberto got his papers in order before the summer, he might want to alternate with her to use the house. His response was a sharp reminder that Roberto was firmly planted between them, and a reality she had to deal with. It was a wake-up call that her marriage was over, no matter how she liked to pretend otherwise to herself occasionally.

Charles was clearly more attached to Roberto than he was to her, and yet he had the audacity to say again that he missed her. In what capacity? As housekeeper and executive assistant to run his home, or to cover for him and make him look good to his children, whom he was only minimally in touch with, between fashionable vacations in Uruguay with Roberto, and trips to Brazil? There was an unreal quality to Charles's life now, and to her own as well, living in the exquisite luxury and history of La Belle Florence in France. There was nothing that she recognized about her life now, nothing familiar about it, and her only local friend was a famous movie star she had only met recently and would probably never see again when they left France.

Ashley picked her up in a battered Citroën "Deux Chevaux" he had found at the château, a car every college student in France had owned at some point in their lives. He swept her an elegant bow, worthy of his early Shakespearean acting career, and helped her into the tiny car, and they drove off to Nemours, twenty-six kilometers away, with a medieval castle. He'd been told there was an excellent *brocante,* and they weren't disappointed. They combed the stalls for hours, and they both found treasures. Ashley had a fondness for antique military uniforms, although most of them were too small for his large frame and broad shoulders, but he found two that fit, with a Napoleonic general's hat that suited him and made them laugh.

Oona found a beautiful lace tablecloth, and an elegant parasol in perfect condition in the palest pink silk that reminded them both of Florence, and Ashley insisted on buying it for her as a gift. They found more recent assorted items to their liking as well, including some 45 rpm records from the sixties, and after packing the spoils of their adventure into the car, they went to the farmer's market nearby to buy produce they didn't have in their gardens. Ashley had planted a vegetable garden of his own at the château during the lockdown and offered to plant one for Oona with her favorite vegetables at La Belle Florence.

They were both hungry for friendship, and were surprised to find that despite their different backgrounds—Ashley's on a tiny island in the Caribbean, with no electricity, surrounded by his large, loving family, and Oona brought up by her widowed mother in New York, going to fancy private schools, and orphaned at an early age in college—they had much in common about their views of life, and how they related to their own children and what was important to them now as adults. Even the eight years between them seemed to make no difference, and the seeds of friendship they planted blossomed quickly into a warm bond of mutual respect that nourished both of them, far from their loved ones and familiar lives in L.A. and New York, despite very different life experiences and careers. Oona was more traditional and Ashley more adventurous, and somehow their differences complemented each other.

Ashley was leery of the glittering superficial life of a star, resisted being pulled into it too deeply, and was realistic about how empty it could be if one trusted it completely or craved it. He had his feet firmly planted on the ground. In time, Oona opened up to him about getting fired from her job of twenty-five years because her less lucrative imprint was being shut down, and over dinner one night, after a few glasses of wine, she told him about Charles falling in love with Roberto, and leaving for Argentina with him, where he was now spending the months of the pandemic while on sabbatical. She trusted Ashley enough to be honest with him, and he didn't disappoint her. He was startled, and sympathetic, and sad for her when she told him the story.

"And you never suspected that he was gay before that?" Ashley looked at her seriously, and she shook her head. "That must have been a hell of a jolt," he said, and she looked pensive, remembering how stunned she had been.

"Maybe I missed the signs, maybe they were there and I didn't want to see them. Looking back, I realize that we started to drift apart a long time ago. We were busy with our careers, and distracted by the kids and what they needed. It's easy to get sidetracked in a marriage after a long time. After a while, we were more friends than lovers, and I'm not even sure exactly when that started. We never had a lot of arguments, we just weren't close, he was always with clients. I was torn between my job and my kids, and I was always running to keep up. We used to have dinner once a week to find out what the other was doing. I guess the dinners were more like debriefings, or scheduling meetings." Ashley didn't feel he knew her well enough to ask her if they still made love, but it was the obvious question, and the answer would have been very rarely. It just didn't have much appeal anymore. She realized now that they were no longer attracted to each other, but she would never have guessed that he would fill that need with a man. She had never asked herself before if he cheated on her and assumed he didn't.

"Maybe it's my fault for not noticing. It's hard to feel sexy when you're always running between your office and your family, or maybe that was just the excuse we used for no longer feeling any attraction to the person we lived with. I thought it was normal after being married for so long. You can't go around asking other people how often they make love, or if they still do, no one I know anyway."

"And now?" Ashley asked her. They were having dinner at the château, accompanied by an excellent bottle of wine Ashley had bought them. Neither of them was drunk, but they were relaxed and more open with each other than usual. "Who do you have now? Is there a man at home in New York?"

She looked him in the eye before she answered. "No. It all happened so fast, from Thanksgiving to Christmas, and then they left for Argentina a few days later. I spent the next six weeks just trying to understand what had happened and get back on my feet mentally and emotionally. I was in no condition to date anyone and didn't want to. And then they announced the merger at work right after the New Year, and everyone was upset. I was worried about my job, but they told me it was secure. Then a month ago, they told me they're closing the small publishing imprint I ran, and now my husband is in Argentina with his boyfriend, so I guess I'm out of that job too. It's hard not to feel like a total flop, but losing the job really isn't my fault—they want to focus on commercial fiction now, and Charles wants to focus on Roberto. I'm not sure if that's my fault or not. It must be in part, since I'm half of the marriage that ran aground. Maybe I treated it more like a job. I was so busy scheduling everyone and everything, I never noticed that he didn't love me anymore. And I didn't love him either, not the way I did in the beginning, and once that's gone, the feeling never comes back again. The relationship changes too much to repair. I was so busy trying to be the most efficient wife and mother in the world, I forgot all about the tenderness of loving someone." She looked sad as she said it, and Ashley felt sorry for her. She was a good person, and a kind woman, and he suspected that she had been a good wife, but with the wrong person, and she was taking a lot of the blame on herself.

"Do you think he had relationships with other men all along?" Ashley found it hard to believe that Charles had only discovered that about himself at fifty-nine.

"He says he didn't, except once in college, but he thought it was an anomaly of some kind, or so he says. At this point, I don't know what to believe—he lied to me for the last year—and maybe it doesn't matter. It is what it is now, and I'll have to deal with it when I go back. As long as I'm away, all of that seems unreal and like it's not happening. At times, I'm really happy here," she admitted, as though there was something wrong with it, "and here, I can pretend that my life won't be completely different when I go home. No job, no husband, my kids thousands of miles away. They have their own lives now, as they should. And so does Charles. The one who has to start from the bottom up again is me. I don't even know where to begin. With a divorce, I guess." She smiled at him ruefully. "Since my kids aren't in New York, I'd rather stay here at La Belle Florence. For now anyway." Oona and Ashley had a warm, cozy evening together, which led to their baring their souls to each other, and he reached across the table and held her hand for a minute. He hadn't done anything like that before, but he was touched by what she told him and how brave and honest she was.

"It's not your fault, Oona. Things happen, people change. You can't blame yourself for his being gay because you were too organized, or worked hard or loved your job, or missed the signals. He must have suspected before Roberto came along. I have a hard time believing he didn't know. And you're a beautiful woman. The fact that you stopped having sex is as much on him as it is on you, maybe more so. Most men wouldn't have let that go. We all make mistakes in our relationships, but I'll bet you made very few. I was the opposite in our marriage. I was too immature to get married. I was twenty-six. Claire and I got involved when we were in drama school together. It was a stormy relationship, off and on after we graduated. I was never faithful to her in the beginning. We were young, we broke up a bunch of times—I was the original bad boy then, and she put up with me. She's a good woman, she just wasn't my woman, and we were too different to ever make it work. My brother told me that before I married her. She hated Trinidad and

Tobago and the Caribbean. She's a typical English girl, from a working-class family in Liverpool, and London was as far as she wanted to go. She's actually done very well—she's had parts in a few good movies, and now she's working in TV in England and she's happy. She thought we'd both be doing Shakespeare forever. When I got the part in the first series, she was terrified it would lead to more and it did. She came to L.A. with me and hated it, and everything my life became after that. Doors opened to me, I got some great parts, and terrific films. She went home to England after a year, and took Alana, my daughter, with her. Claire didn't want her to grow up in L.A. She was pregnant again when she left—I think she did it on purpose, and she thought that would force me to give up L.A. I went back to London with her for a while. I was faithful to her by then and tried to be a decent husband. But we had too much bad history between us, too much to overcome. She was angry at me for the eight years before that and she couldn't let it go. I don't blame her, but we shouldn't have gotten married. Marriage doesn't fix a shaky relationship. It makes it worse. It's the great magnifier of whatever is there. It doesn't change it. When she had Simon, my son, I wanted her to come back with the kids to L.A., and she refused. I wanted the career L.A. could give me. I wanted both my family and the career I had. I wanted it all. I wanted to work in England and L.A. and have my wife and kids with me. She wouldn't do it—she hated it when my career took off, and she filed for divorce. Maybe I should have stayed in England, but I would have resented forever what I had to give up. Just working in England wouldn't have been enough for me, once I got a taste for the kind of work I could get in L.A. I had so many great opportunities. It was too much to give up for her. She basically divorced me because of my success. Her boyfriend now owns a restaurant in Notting Hill, and she's as happy as can be. She hated what my career turned into, so now I fly back to London to see my kids, and have them come to me, and visit my family in Trinidad when I can, and I'm happy. I wanted to seize the opportunities I was given, but I feel bad when I can't be there for my kids. I try to see them as much as I can." Oona could tell he loved his children deeply and felt guilty for the time he missed with them, but he had a fabulous career too. He'd had chances no one would turn down, and was still a good person, and a kind, honorable man.

"It sounds like you're doing a good job of having both, the kids and your work. It would have been a shame to give up the career you have. You're an amazing actor, Ashley. You can't keep a talent like that hidden or chained to the wall. You'd have been miserable if you gave that up. The older your kids get, the more time they'll probably spend with you. How old are they?"

"Simon's six, and a little devil"—he grinned when he said it—"and Alana is almost a lady now, she's twelve. Her mother got pregnant as soon as we got married. I think she thought that would tie me down and anchor me, and apparently nothing does." He smiled and she laughed. He was like a big, beautiful bird who needed to fly away at times, but always came back to his nest, and his family, in the end. But he couldn't be caged. She could sense that about him. "I'd love you to meet my kids sometime," he added. They were truly friends now. The stresses of the pandemic had strengthened their bond and they had no distractions from each other. Ashley spoke to his agent almost daily, but he wasn't present with her in Milly-la-Forêt.

"I'd love you to meet mine. Will goes down to L.A. a lot, but Meghan is a long way from home now, loving what she does. I don't know when she'll come home. Will is much more of a home-body than she is. She needs big skies, like you." She smiled at him, and he could see that she understood. They were very accepting of each other. Oona suspected it was because they were just friends. The moment there was more involved, in the high-stakes game of love, when all the chips were on the table, when you risked every-thing, that was when the heavy losses happened.

"Do you want to get married again?" he asked her, curious, and she shook her head.

"I put in twenty-five years and got fired," she said with a rueful smile. "I don't want to go through that ever again."

"You didn't get fired," he corrected her, "you got laid off, the firm went out of business. It sounds to me like your husband was emotionally bankrupt. Maybe you just outgrew each other. That happens. Twenty-five years is a damn good run. It's awfully hard to find someone who will suit you twenty-five years later. You grow up and things change. You don't always grow in the same direction as the person you live with—in fact it's extremely rare."

"I realize that now," she said. "Charles and I outgrew each other years ago. We don't like any of the same things today. Sometimes I miss the man he used to be, but I don't miss who he is now." Ash-ley nodded, he understood. He felt the same way about his ex-wife.

"When I see Claire now, I wonder how we were ever together.

We have nothing in common either. We have nothing to talk about now, except the kids."

"That sounds like the last fifteen years of my marriage," she said.

Ashley took her home after dinner and they went to stroll in the gardens.

Oona loved thinking about the king and his beloved mistress, walking the same path centuries before. It was so easy talking to Ashley, and just being with him. She was so grateful to have him as a friend. She hoped they would stay friends when they left France, but the one thing the last seven months had taught her, and especially the pandemic, was that nothing was predictable anymore. You could never guess what the future had in store.

Chapter 7

Ashley and Oona fell into an easy rhythm through all of June, alternating lunches at her house, with dinners at the château. He had the better kitchen, with enormous spaces, excellent appliances, and tools he used well. He made them some fabulous meals, of Caribbean and French cooking. It was fun to see what he would cook next. He had bought some Indian and Asian cookbooks, and was learning to prepare their delicacies too. He was an excellent chef, along with his other talents. He enjoyed cooking for her.

Ashley planted a vegetable garden for Oona, as he had promised, and she loved watching the things that he had planted grow. They lay at her pool sometimes, relaxing, and then he'd make lunch for them, or they played tennis in the late afternoon at the château. They were evenly matched at some things, and she loved playing tennis with him. She'd never had a friendship like this with a man, even in college and before she was married. They laughed and they played cards—they both loved to play poker. She had no need to compete with him. She beat him at cards, and he excelled at athletics. They went running together. They visited châteaux and monuments and museums. He had a passion for history. They went riding together. He had learned to ride for one of his movies and loved it. Sometimes they walked through the woods in comfortable silence, enjoying the small animals they saw, and listening to the birds. Life at La Belle Florence was peaceful.

The Covid numbers had improved, although they'd both heard that people were being too relaxed in the south of France, partying and crowding onto the beaches, not wearing masks. They all desperately needed to forget the stress of the life they had lived for the past six months. They had been vigilant night and day, determined to survive the damage and anxiety of the pandemic, transforming fear to courage. There was a constant drumbeat of stress in the distance, like a war. It was impossible to ignore it.

Experiencing it together day by day brought Ashley and Oona closer. They knew each other well now. They were conscious of their differences and respectful of them. And in the isolation they lived in, color didn't matter to them or the people around them. He was a major star, which gave him carte blanche in real life. They were aware that they got a free pass that others didn't because of who he was, and he was gracious to everyone they encountered. He handled every situation with patience, intelligence, poise, and grace. And Oona was aware that being his friend was an honor and a privilege, which she respected. He was a person of principles. They both were.

Oona had talked to Gail in New York about her friendship with Ashley Rowe. All the employees of the newly enlarged Hargrove

Publishing—combined with Shipsted and Breck, dangerously close to a monopoly now—were still working remotely from home, as was Will at Google. Giant corporations were functioning by Zoom and similar applications online. Better summer weather had boosted spirits everywhere and was also causing the Covid figures to rise, as people went out more and socialized, which continued to cause the virus to spread. But people were a little more light-hearted than they had been in the winter months, hibernating in isolation, and in many cases unable to see their loved ones. The pandemic was taking a heavy toll, particularly on the young and the elderly, who were sequestered more than other age groups. Divorce, child abuse, domestic violence, and suicide were on the rise, and statistically alarming. The U.S. was one of the hardest hit countries, with fragmented authority between mayors, governors, and health officials, all contradicting each other. No two cities, states, or counties had the same rules, with a broad range of protocols, from no acknowledgment of the virus at all to total lockdown. The virus was having a field day.

Gail acknowledged to Oona that she was sick and tired of being stuck in her apartment, on Zoom meetings all day to keep her department running. The anticipated firings had taken place, and hundreds of employees of both merged houses had been let go. Many hadn't been replaced and the newly formed company was operating with a smaller staff than they intended to employ in future. It was brutally hard to train new people, particularly those in first-time jobs, on screen and at a distance. Everything was harder than it had been "before." And the first available vaccines were still months away. It wasn't an easy situation for anyone. And Ashley and Oona were not exempt from the stress and restrictions in Milly-la-Forêt, the surroundings were just prettier.

Gail was stunned and impressed by Oona's friendship with a major Hollywood star who was everyone's idol and publicly acknowledged as a wonderful human being by all who knew him. "Some people have all the luck," Gail growled at her, as Oona sat on her terrace overlooking the exquisitely manicured garden at the end of her day, while Gail was eating a sandwich and yogurt during her lunch break. Gail was wearing an old Chanel jacket she had bought at a resale shop years before, with frayed denim shorts and furry bedroom slippers, because all anyone could see on Zoom was the serious black Chanel jacket, worthy of a department head of HSB—Hargrove, Shipsted and Breck. No one could see the shorts or the fluffy slippers. Oona could see that Gail's hair had grown almost to her shoulders and had gone gray. She said she hadn't had a decent haircut since February. The hairdresser she loved had moved home to New Hampshire, and the salon Gail always went to was closed. She wasn't unique in her complaints. "I can't believe it," Gail commented. "You get stuck in France in what looks like Cinderella's castle,"—Oona had shown her parts of La Belle Florence on FaceTime, including the vegetable garden Ashley had planted for her, from which she ate every day—"your new best friend is one of the best-looking actors in America, and you pal around every day, visiting yard sales and châteaux and playing cards with him at night after he cooks a three-star dinner for you, and the most exciting thing that's happened to me in months is that the guy where I buy my bagels gave me free cream cheese yesterday, and a free bagel last week. There are no movie stars at my house," she said glumly, and then she smiled at her friend on their computer screens, "but I'm happy for you. You deserve it. What happens to the friendship after the pandemic, if we all live long enough to see the end?" she asked Oona.

"He goes back to his life between London and L.A. making movies and series, and I go back to mine in New York and look for a job as an editor. I hope we'll see each other when he comes through New York on location or for a premiere of one of his movies. I have to admit, I'll miss him. It's nice having a friend here, it makes the whole thing bearable," she said with a sigh.

"So why can't that continue after?" Gail asked bluntly.

"Because we don't live in the same city and I'm not his girl-friend."

"Why not? You're a beautiful woman. You're smart, you're fun, you're well educated. You get along with everyone. You're a nice person."

"For one thing, I'm married," Oona said. Gail interrupted her immediately.

"To a man who is probably taking tango lessons with his boy-friend in Buenos Aires. You're not 'married' in the true sense of the word. Only legally."

"Ashley and I don't have that kind of relationship. We're pals, as it should be. I'm eight years older than he is."

"And you don't look it," Gail said stubbornly.

"He has a very glamorous life, I don't. He has dated the hottest young actresses in Hollywood."

"So what. He'll outgrow them. He won't outgrow you. Is color an issue?" Gail asked Oona directly. She had wondered about it before and hadn't asked her.

Oona answered her thoughtfully. "Not for us. I never think about it, and I don't think he does either. But others might, or probably would," Oona said seriously. "Ashley isn't angry. He's a happy, well-balanced person. He had a wonderful childhood and loves his family. That makes a difference."

"Your kids?" Gail was curious. Neither woman had ever had an interracial relationship before. It didn't happen much or at all in Oona's bourgeois Park Avenue social circles, and it had never happened in Gail's either when she was younger. She'd gone out with a Black attorney for a while, and once a Black author, but it still didn't happen to her often.

"No, my kids wouldn't care. Meghan would be thrilled—she has a huge crush on him. Kids of that generation don't see color. It all looks the same to them. I don't know about his kids, they're very young. He's dated other white women. I just think generally in public people react to it. There is still a huge issue with racism in the States. No one seems to care that much about it here. Famous Black Americans have been moving to France since the forties and fifties. It's not about that for us. The public loves Ashley—even here, everyone recognizes him. It's just that relationships of any color are complicated. He had a bad marriage, I'm about to have a bad divorce. We started out as friends, and we're comfortable with it. I think the age difference is a bigger deal. He doesn't need to drag some old bag around. That's how people would see it."

"That's crap. You're forty-seven, not ninety-two, and you don't look your age. You look the same age as he does. Is he upset about your age?" Gail didn't like the sound of that.

"It's not an issue since we're only friends. He's much too polite to mention it. And as friends, I could be ninety and it wouldn't matter. It's fine like this."

"Eight years is nothing, for God's sake," Gail said, frustrated. "Men fall in love with women ten and twenty years older, just as women do. It's who you are and how you feel, what you believe in, and share. I never heard you sound like this about Charles. And just because he screwed you over, you can't decide that you're too old for someone to love you. You're still young, Oona. Don't waste it."

"I'm not. We have a fantastic time together, and we get along incredibly well. Whatever the difference in how we grew up, we see things the same way."

"Do you know how rare that is?" Gail insisted. She wanted her friend to be happy, and not miss the chance, by limiting it to friendship. She was convinced that there was more there, and Oona was refusing to see it or open the door to it. It sounded to her like Ashley was in love with her.

"I know it is. He's amazing, but he'll be going back to L.A. after all this, and I'll be back in New York. And he's a big star everywhere. I'm nobody."

"Your kids aren't here anymore, your husband is in love with a guy in Argentina, you're not at Hargrove anymore. What are you coming back to New York for?" Gail's argument was a good one.

"To see you of course! And look for another job in publishing."

"Why? This place has been miserable since the merger. And all the big houses are the same. They lose their humanity when they get this big. It's not fun anymore. They don't care who works here, or even who they publish. We're just numbers to them, and part of the bottom line. I've been here as long as you were, and sometimes I wonder if they even know who I am," Gail said, sounding forlorn.

"Publishing is all I know," Oona said. She'd been thinking about it a lot herself. Whenever she knew she was going back, she was going to call the headhunters again, to set up interviews for her, but they would undoubtedly complain that she had no experience with commercial fiction, and there was a limited market for debut literary fiction. They would want her to go out and find new authors of commercial fiction to groom for bestsellers. She wasn't sure she had the right instincts for it.

"Maybe you should write a book. Have you ever thought of that?"

"I don't know that I have the talent. I doubt it. I've been painting lately—I started in the confinement—but Picasso I'm not. To be honest, I'm not sure who I am anymore, or what I should be doing. I obviously blew it as a wife, now I've lost my job. All the markers I relied on to define my identity have disappeared. Even my kids don't need me anymore."

"In a way, that must be very liberating. You don't have to be anything you don't want to be, a wife, a hands-on mother, a publisher in a category that's fairly limited in readership in a market that is ruled by big bestsellers and greedy publishers. Maybe you should do something completely different. Do you even *want* to come back to New York, and if so, why? As well as closing some doors, which I'll admit is painful, maybe this can open some doors too. And that includes your next relationship. Why not be with a younger man, or a movie star, or whoever makes you happy and excites you and inspires you. And the same about your job. For the first time in years, you have a totally clean slate. Maybe that's what you need to look at, and figure out what you want to write on it. Don't limit yourself by the past or what other people think. Screw them. Figure out what *you* want. You've earned it, Oona. The good thing about being our age is that you've paid your dues. So now you get to pick, the man, the place, the job, whatever you want." What Gail said was inspiring. Oona could always count on Gail for that. Gail looked at her watch then. "Shit, I have a Zoom meeting in ten minutes. Finance committee, to assess what my department will make this year. That's all they care about now. Ever since the merger. Be happy you're not here. I would trade places with you in a hot minute."

"Thank you," Oona said with a warm smile. "I think I needed to hear that. I guess I do have some options."

"Go get 'em. We'll celebrate with a bagel when you get back. The cream cheese is on me." Oona laughed. Ashley was going to make a mushroom soufflé at the château that night, from an Alain Ducasse recipe he had found online. He had even taught Oona to make a few things herself, and she'd enjoyed it. She had mastered the art of Hollandaise sauce. He had a fail-safe recipe he had shared with her, to go with the asparagus from his garden. They were wholesome pastimes they both enjoyed, like so many things they did together. But she still thought Gail was crazy to assume they had a future together as a couple. Oona was sure it hadn't even crossed Ashley's mind, or hers. She cherished him as a friend and respected him profoundly. It was an honor to be close to him, and a privilege. She didn't want to screw it up with a romance that wouldn't last and had no future. He would go back to dating his famous movie stars when he went back to L.A. But in the meantime, she loved what they shared, and didn't expect more from him, nor did he expect anything more of her, she was sure of it.

She arrived at the château at eight o'clock, as she always did. There was no light on in the kitchen, which was unusual. He was supposed to be putting together the ingredients for the soufflé. She called out his name and he answered from upstairs where his suite was. She walked up the stairs, until she saw his bedroom. The door was open, there was a small suitcase on the bed and he was packing. He looked up when she reached the doorway, and saw that he was worried. He was moving fast, throwing things into the bag, socks, underwear, a pair of loafers. He was wearing sneakers, jeans, a white shirt, and a dark blue linen blazer.

"Are you going somewhere?" she asked him. It was obvious he was. He talked to her as he continued to pack.

"I got a call from Claire's sister an hour ago. Claire is sick. With Covid. She got sick five days ago. Alana said something to me about it a few days ago. She wasn't too bad then. Alana asked me if I thought she'd go to the hospital, and I said I didn't think so, so now she'll think I'm a liar, as well as an absentee dad. I haven't seen them in three months because of the quarantine, which was very strict. You had to isolate for two weeks on arrival. They just changed the regulations literally days ago, so I won't have to now, fortunately, just have a negative Covid test. The kids' mother had scarlet fever as a child, and she has a heart murmur. She has a pacemaker, and somewhat fragile health, so she's in the high-risk category. She tested positive a few days ago, and she's sick now. It sounds like she got bad pretty fast. She had trouble breathing last night, and they took her to the hospital this morning. Apparently, she's not doing well—they're talking about intubating her. They won't let anyone see her at the hospital, so I can't see her, but the kids are very upset. I'm going to see them. They're both in quarantine too, having been in contact with their mother." He looked deadly serious for a moment. "I should be there in case anything happens. I hope she'll be all right. I want to see the kids. I'll be careful and wear a mask with them of course. They tested negative, and they'll have to be tested again. They haven't been with her since she developed symptoms, but she was contagious before that. Hopefully they'll be okay."

Oona looked at him for a moment. He was distracted and obviously upset. He had put ten pairs of socks into his rolling bag, while she watched him, and didn't hesitate with her next question.

"Do you want me to come with you?" she asked. It was an honest offer. He smiled a small, wintry smile and shook his head.

"Thank you. There's nothing you can do, but I appreciate it."

"I can wait at a hotel, so I'm there if you need me." He stopped what he was doing and looked at her more seriously.

"Thank you, Oona. You can't. If you come with me, you can't get back into France with an American passport. I have a visa for France the studio got me, for the series I was supposed to be making. It's a long-term visa for famous people in creative fields called a 'Talent Passport,' and I have a British passport as well as my American one. With just an American passport, you can't get back in here once you leave, while the borders are closed. But I appreciate the offer. I'll call and let you know what's happening," he promised, and then he looked apologetic, and gave her a hug. "Will you take a rain check for the soufflé?" he asked her, and she smiled, worried about him and his children. They were young, and what if they lost their mother? She hoped they wouldn't. She remembered how deeply shaken she had been at eighteen when her mother died. "I'm sorry I didn't call you to cancel dinner. I've been rushing like a madman since Claire's sister called. The kids are very upset." It was a terrible wake-up call as to how dangerous the virus was. Oona was sorry she couldn't go with him, just to be in the area, even if she couldn't see him, but she didn't want to get locked out of France.

They went down to the kitchen then, and he carried his rolling bag. He glanced at his watch. "I have a car coming in half an hour. I'm staying at Claire's. You can reach me on my cell. Normally, her boyfriend is there, but he's going back to his own place so I can be with my kids. He's a decent chap and he loves her. They've been together for four or five years now. They got together fairly soon after we separated. He's good to my kids, and to her, and very civil to me." Ashley made himself a quick sandwich and had finished it by the time the car arrived. Oona walked him to the car, and he gave her a hug and kissed her lightly on the mouth. He'd never done that before and she was surprised. He was touched that she had offered to go with him. "Be good while I'm gone. I'll call you," he promised when the car came, and she waved as they pulled away and drove across the drawbridge. There was still a moat around the château that had been there since it was built in the sixteenth century. Château Bertigny had once been a fortress, which protected its inhabitants during sieges by their enemies.

When Ashley had left, Oona got back in her car and drove back to La Belle Florence, and she felt a sudden void the moment he was gone. It was so comforting to always know he was nearby. She hoped that everything would go well in London and his ex-wife would be okay.

She spent a quiet evening with the dog, watching one of her favorite shows, and went to sleep early. Ashley texted her when he arrived in London. She sent him her good thoughts again. And she had another message from him when she woke up in the morning. He said only that nothing had changed.

She worked on one of her paintings while he was away and called Will. He and Heather were working remotely, and they sounded fine. Talking to Will made Oona miss them more. She hadn't heard from Meghan for a few days, but she knew that she was busy. She missed Ashley but she didn't want to call him and intrude if it was a bad time and he was with the kids. He called her late that night when they were asleep and reported that their mother wasn't doing well and was in the ICU. He said she was having a lot of trouble breathing, and they were going to intubate her if she didn't improve, which didn't sound good to Oona.

She worked on the painting some more to pass the time, and was thinking about Ashley and his children when she went to bed that night. She had no news when she woke up in the morning, and walked to the vegetable garden he had planted, to get some things for lunch.

She called him late that afternoon, which was an hour earlier for him in London, but he didn't pick up, so she sent him a text instead, hoping that things were going well. She was worried when she went to bed that night with no news. In the morning she read a text from him that she had feared. Claire's heart had given out early that morning, and she had died of cardiac arrest. She was a year younger than Ashley and had died of Covid. Ashley said he would call Oona when he could. His children were devastated. Oona had a heavy heart all day when she thought about them. It brought her own mother's death back vividly. She could easily imagine how distraught they felt, and they were much younger than she had been when her mother died. She knew Ashley would be deeply saddened too. The marriage hadn't worked, but she was the mother of his children, and he had loved her once, and he always said that she was a good mother and a good person. It was terrible news, and Claire was the first person Oona knew at close range who had died of Covid-19. She was another tragic statistic in the world crisis that was continuing to unfold. Oona didn't hear from Ashley for two days and could well imagine he had his hands full with his kids and Claire's grieving family. They were only allowed to have ten people at the funeral, and as soon as it was over, he called her and sounded very subdued.

"Are you okay?" she asked him in a somber tone.

"More or less." He sounded terrible.

"I'm so sorry, that's so awful."

"It attacked her heart. They tried to bring her back but they couldn't." He sounded desperately sad, for Claire, and his children.

"How are the kids doing?"

"Simon is doing better than Alana, but I'm not sure he fully gets it yet. The family is just destroyed. I'm bringing the children back to France with me tomorrow. I can get them in on my visa at their age. They need a change of scene, and I want them with me. We're flying private. I don't want to take any risks with them."

"Do you need me to get anything ready for them? I don't want to intrude. I'll just leave whatever you need at Bertigny, so it's there when you arrive. Are there any foods they like?" It touched him that she wanted to comfort his children. Alana was heartbroken to have lost her mother, and that she never got to say goodbye. Simon looked dazed and had wet his bed the night before. Ashley knew how much they would need him now, and he was glad he wasn't working, and could spend all his time with them.

"I can't think of anything they'd want to eat. I'll make them pizza or something. This is going to be so tough for them."

"I know," Oona said sympathetically. "I went through it, and I was older than they are. Let me know if you think of anything I can do."

"I called the housekeeper and told her what room to get ready for Alana. I'll have Simon sleep with me. He's prone to nightmares anyway, and this won't help." Even Ashley had a hard time believing that Claire was gone. He kept getting flashbacks of their wedding, of when she was pregnant, of when Alana and Simon were born. So many scenes crowded into his mind. He had known Claire since he was eighteen and she was seventeen, when they went to school together after he first arrived in London. Their marriage hadn't been a success, but he had loved her as a sister and a friend and a special person in his life, and he knew he always would. There were tears in his eyes when he hung up with Oona, and he was glad he had her to return to in Milly-la-Forêt.

When the children were feeling a little less shell-shocked, he wanted to introduce them to Oona, just as a friend, and he was counting on her excellent motherly advice. He considered her an authority on the subject—since she was so attentive to her own children, he was sure she would be good with his. He was grateful that she was a mature person, and not some twenty-two-year-old starlet obsessed with herself and unable to relate to his kids. Oona was just who they needed to help them. He sent her a text immediately, thanking her for her help, and he signed it "love, Ash," which was a first for him. She interpreted it as a gesture of friendship, despite everything Gail had said, guessing that he was in love with her. Oona still didn't think so, but that wasn't important right now. All that mattered to her and Ashley was comforting Alana and Simon and giving them all the love and nurturing they needed.

She fell asleep thinking of them that night, and of their mother, and Ashley. Her heart went out to all of them. When she woke up in the morning, her pillow was wet with tears. For the first time in a long time, she had been crying for her mother, and theirs too.

Chapter 8

The Château Bertigny distracted Alana and Simon when they first arrived. They'd never been in a private jet before. Simon was allowed to sit in a jump seat in the cockpit after takeoff, and he loved it and said he wanted to be a pilot when he grew up, or a baseball player, or a fireman. The pilot had a grandson his age, and explained to him what some of the controls were, and then Simon went back to his father and sister, and had something to eat before they landed at Le Bourget near Paris. A van and driver were waiting to take them to Milly-la-Forêt, and Ashley told them about the history of the château. Simon was excited to see it. Alana just sat in her seat and stared out the window, thinking of her mother. She was wearing a short black skirt, a white blouse, and ballerina flats, with her dark hair in curls down her back. It killed Ashley to see the look in her eyes, and he held her hand for most of the trip, while Simon chatted with the driver and told him all about the plane. He fell asleep before they got there—he had been up since dawn. Alana didn't say a word on the trip from the airport. Ashley was worried about her, and wondered how long it would take for her to begin to recover from the shock of her mother's death, or for any of them. Ashley was feeling it too. He felt as though he had been beaten up the day before, ever since the funeral. Ashley and the children had been there with Claire's family. It was brief and small, according to Covid rules. And excruciating. Alana had looked like she was in shock, and Simon cried. And so did Ashley. Claire's family was devastated. She was only thirty-eight.

Alana revived a little when they walked into the château and Ashley took her to her room. It was the closest guest room to his, all done in pink Toile de Jouy with trees and shepherd girls and country scenes woven into the fabric. He showed her how close his own room was, and set Simon's things down in his room, to unpack later. Ashley let them settle into their rooms, and then took them downstairs for the lunch the housekeeper had made. Alana barely touched hers, and Simon ate half the sandwich, some cookies and some cherries.

"What are we doing this afternoon, Dad?" Simon asked him, and Ashley said they could take a walk around and wade in the stream near the house.

"Can we go swimming?" Simon asked him. "Do we have a pool?"

"No, but we have a friend who does, a few miles from here. And she has horses too."

"Can we go now?"

"Maybe tomorrow," he said, glancing at Alana. She was in no shape to visit anyone. He wanted to be gentle with her and give her the time and space she needed right now. In the end, they took a walk in the gardens, and he showed them the stream. Simon took his shoes and socks off, and waded in it, walking from rock to rock with his father holding his hand, while Alana sat down on a rock and watched them. She didn't join them, and then they went back to the château and she went to her room to finish unpacking her things, and Simon bounded out to the kitchen for some more of the cookies the housekeeper had made. Ashley went out to the terrace and called Oona on his cell.

"Are you here?" she asked him.

"I am. We arrived this morning. There isn't a lot for them to do at the château." He had realized it when he walked them around. "Can we come and visit you tomorrow?" he asked. "Simon wants to go swimming, and it would be good for Alana too. I'm sorry to ask. I don't know what to do for them."

"You can ask or come over anytime. How is Alana doing?"

"About the way you'd expect. She looks so sad, it breaks my heart every time I see her." It was normal, but agony to watch.

"Why don't you come before lunch tomorrow? They can swim, and then we'll have lunch. They can ride in the afternoon if they want. We could ride with them. Do they ride?"

"They do. I don't know if Alana will want to, but Simon will. He's bursting at the seams with energy, even though he's sad too."

"It's going to take time," Oona said wisely. She didn't ask him how long the children were staying, because she suspected he didn't know yet. It was all too fresh. "Why don't you come at eleven tomorrow, and I'll figure out something to eat." She didn't want him to have to make any effort. He was in mourning too. "Can I do anything for you and them tonight?"

"No, I just want to give them time to get their bearings and relax. I'll be happy to see you tomorrow," he said to Oona. "It's been a rough few days."

"I know," she said gently. "I'll be happy to see you too."

She had an idea after they spoke. She had seen some things at the general store in the village that might be good for Simon, and maybe even Alana. She got in her car, drove the short distance, parked in front, and went in with her mask on. They had inflatable pool toys in boxes on a shelf, and they were still there. She brought six of them to the counter: a big white swan, a giant yellow duck like a mammoth bath toy, a hamburger, a unicorn, a seahorse, and a dolphin. She got a big beach ball, and a soccer ball for Ash and Simon. There were assorted toys and games. She bought a croquet set and another deck of cards than the one she and Ashley played with, and a big puzzle of a country scene for Alana, and another one of butterflies, and some easy ones for Simon. It was enough to keep them busy for quite a while. And before she left the store, she bought a sketch pad and colored pencils. She put it all in the car and drove home, going right to the stables so the stable hands could fill the pool toys with air. She got everything ready for the next day, tossing the inflatable toys into the water, where they floated regally on the surface, waiting for the Rowe children to show up. She set the games on the table on the terrace and went inside to make sure that the groceries she'd gotten had been put in the fridge.

She set the table for the next day, with a royal blue tablecloth and yellow and blue plates and yellow napkins, and cut blue, yellow, and red flowers in the garden and put them in a vase in the center of the table. She wanted it to look festive and happy for Ashley's children.

She called him at nine o'clock that evening, and he sounded tired and said the children were already in bed and asleep. He couldn't wait to see her the next day. They talked for a while, and then he said he was going to bed too.

When Ashley drove up the driveway and stopped outside the house, Oona came out to greet them, with Florence running along beside her. She barked at them for a few minutes and Simon jumped out of the car to pet the little dog. She wagged her tail frantically, running around in a circle, and when he kneeled down to pet her, she licked his face and he glanced up at his father, beaming.

"What's her name?" Simon asked Oona, and she smiled at him, and then at Alana, who was wearing a pink denim skirt and a white T-shirt and sandals, and carrying their bathing suits in a bag.

"Her name is Florence, and mine is Oona, and I'm happy to meet you," she said.

"That's a funny name," Simon said, grinning, and she noticed that he was missing his two front teeth. He was a beautiful child and looked like his father. Alana looked more like her mother, with delicate Ethiopian features.

"Yes, it is a funny name," she agreed. "Florence likes you." Simon picked her up then, and she kissed his face again and he laughed and set her down gently on her feet, and Oona thanked Alana for coming. She had lemonade and cookies on the terrace for them, and she took them around to the changing rooms next to the pool, where they disappeared into the cabana with the bag, Alana taking charge of her brother.

"They're gorgeous children," Oona said to Ashley, and he smiled and gave her a hug.

"Thank you. I missed you. It's been an awful week." She nodded, poured a glass of lemonade, and handed it to him, and he drank it gladly. It was a hot day. They waited for the children to come out in their bathing suits. Alana had a little pink two-piece bathing suit, and Simon had a royal blue one with dolphins on it, and Alana grinned and Simon screamed with delight when they saw the pool toys. He jumped into the pool, while Alana walked in from the shallow end, and for the next hour and a half they played like normal children who hadn't lost their mother three days before. It warmed Ashley's heart and Oona's to see them playing.

"Did you get all that for them?" he asked her, and she nodded.

"I thought they needed a little fun," she said softly, and he gave her a grateful look.

She made them pizza and a salad for lunch, with ice cream bars for dessert. They went back to the pool afterward, swam for a while, and lay in the sun to dry off, and then they went to see the horses. Simon loved them, and Alana said she liked to ride, and they decided to come back the next day to ride with Oona and their father. Oona told Ash she would put Simon on a lead line— she had picked a pony for him, and a very tame small horse for Alana.

The children played some of the games after they saw the

horses, and Ashley and Oona chatted a little distance away from them. It had been a good day for the kids, and the adults too.

"You're amazing with them," he whispered to her.

"They're lovely children. Will they stay here now?" He nodded. "Claire's family isn't equipped to take care of them. Her parents are too old, her sister is sweet but she's a flake and her husband drinks too much. I have to figure things out now. I don't want them to live like nomads with me. I'm not really set up for kids at the moment, without their mother. I'll have to make some adjustments when I go back to L.A. One of my sisters has offered to take them in Trinidad and she has kids the same age, but I think they need to be with me, now that their mother isn't here to take care of them. It's fine here this summer, but when we go back to the States, I'll have to figure it out. I promised them I would. They want to stay with me, so that's what we'll do."

"You're lucky," Oona said to Ashley, remembering her own children at the same age. She missed that, and the good times they'd had together when they were younger. It made her think that maybe she'd been lucky that Charles hadn't made his big discoveries earlier. At least Meghan and Will had had their father around for the important years when they were growing up. What he was doing now didn't have an impact on them the way it would have had when they were younger. They had their own lives now. The one who had to rebuild her life was Oona. But she didn't want to think about that now.

She and Ashley took a swim in the pool while the children were playing with the puzzles she'd bought. She'd bought easy ones for Simon, and Alana was working on the one with the butterflies.

Oona had put it on a game board so they could take it inside later and she could finish it another time. They all played a round of Clue before Ashley and the children left. Oona helped them get their belongings together, and they decided to leave their swimsuits so they could come and swim the next day, and ride the horses. She stood and watched Ashley with his children for a few minutes. He was so gentle and loving with them, and he glanced up and saw her and smiled at her.

"Thank you for a perfect day," he said to her, as Simon popped up between them and looked at her.

"Are you my dad's girlfriend?" he asked her, and Ashley and Oona exchanged a glance as she shook her head.

"No, Simon, I'm not. We're just good friends and you can visit whenever you want, and swim and feed the horses, and ride. Florence and I will be happy to see you anytime."

"You're nice," he complimented her, and then Alana helped him into the car, and they all waved as they drove away. It had all turned out even better than she'd hoped, and they had enjoyed everything she bought for them. Simon had done a drawing of Florence and had given it to Oona as a gift. The children warmed her heart, and she was smiling when she took the pitcher of lemonade inside and put it in the fridge.

Ashley called her again that night after the children went to bed.

"Thank you for making it such a special day for them. It was like a birthday party, and they were the honored guests."

"All three of you were," she told him.

"It felt like it. Simon was still talking about you when he fell asleep. He wore himself out—he'll sleep like a baby tonight." He was sleeping in Ashley's bed.

"So will Florence," Oona said with a laugh. She was already sound asleep on Oona's bed, waiting for her and snoring. She liked her new life.

"I hope I can do a decent job of it for them, when I take them to L.A. I've only had them for short visits on my own. Their mother was better at the day-to-day stuff than I was, keeping all their activities and lessons straight."

"You should get someone to help you. You can't do it all yourself, especially when you go back to work."

"How did you manage that, with a job, a husband, and a family?"

"Looking back, I have no idea how I did it. All it took was a lot of energy, and no sleep."

"I don't know how women do it," he said, in awe of her, and all the treats she had provided for them in the past twenty-four hours. Oona had given Alana one of the puzzles to take with her, to do at the château. She left the butterfly one at Oona's to work on the next time she was there. "Thank you for buying all those things to entertain them." It was all a bit overwhelming, even for Oona. Ashley said they had loved it all, and her, and couldn't wait to come back the next day. Simon considered her his property now, and Alana was emerging slowly. Oona had helped her shower after the pool, and wash her hair, which her mother had always done. Oona could see how sad Alana was from the stricken look on her face, and afterward, she thanked Oona politely.

Ashley wished her goodnight then. Simon was already sound

asleep, and he cuddled up next to him when Ashley got into bed. He was thinking of Oona and what a remarkable woman she was, and how lucky he was to have met her.

They came back the next day and swam again, and Ashley made lunch that time. They all swam in the pool and played games, and they rode at the end of the day, and Oona smiled as she watched them leave. She knew they still missed their mother, but they were enjoying their visits to Oona, and Ashley was grateful for her help. They baked her a chocolate cake that night at the château and brought it to her proudly the next day. Alana had done the icing, and Simon had added sprinkles, and Ashley had written "Thank you, Oona" on the cake. Oona took pictures of it with her phone, and then they ate it.

For all of July and August, swimming at her house became a daily ritual, and Simon helped her pick vegetables in the garden. Oona put pale pink nail polish on Alana's toes, the way she had on Meghan's at the same age, just for fun. She had told them about her children and showed them photographs of them. Alana had told her all about her aunt in Trinidad who was sixteen and really cool.

"That's my youngest sister, Olivia," Ashley explained to Oona.

"I guessed." She smiled at him.

They were still at the château at the end of August, as the days began to cool. Schools were still closed in California, so Ashley wasn't rushing to go back. He needed to enroll them in a school in

L.A., and then they would attend classes remotely. It was a less-than-ideal situation academically, and they'd been through it in England with schools closed from March through May and just recently reopened in June.

Their father and Oona took the children to Euro Disney with their masks on, and went to Paris for the day and showed them the sights. They couldn't go up the Eiffel Tower, but they went to the top of the Arc de Triomphe and looked all the way down the Champs-Élysées, and they had tea and macarons at an outdoor café. Both children slept all the way back to Milly-la-Forêt. They had walked for hours, and they loved the city, but they were happy to be back in Oona's pool the next day, as Florence sat on the edge and played lifeguard, watching them intently, and barking when they splashed each other.

Oona had dinner with them at the château and left later than usual one night, after the children went to bed, so she and Ashley had some quiet time to talk. When he walked her to the car, through the garden, he stopped and kissed her, with a big orange harvest moon in the sky overhead. It was a slow searing kiss, and she responded. It was the first time he had kissed her.

"I've been wanting to do that for months," he whispered, and she had too, but she was worried about it. She thought about it all the way back to her house. She didn't want to do anything that would spoil their friendship. Things were so perfect as they were. But he was so beautiful, gentle and kind, and being with him was so intoxicating and so comfortable, and she was falling in love with his children too. Being with Ashley in France was like being on a desert island, and real life as they knew it had been eclipsed by the pandemic. The lives they had been living had vanished six months before.

She lay in her bed that night, thinking about him, not sure what to do. Sooner or later, they would all go home. Ashley and his children would go back to L.A., and she'd be alone in New York, and she didn't want to do anything now that she'd regret later, but it was so hard to resist. And every day could have been their last if they got sick. She didn't want to turn her back on her feelings for Ashley and his children. But everything about the future was so unsure. And what kind of future could they ever have together?

The children were playing in the pool the next day, as Oona and Ashley watched them from a distance, and he looked at her carefully. He could see how frightened she was. They had crossed a line the night before when he kissed her, and entered new, unfamiliar territory.

"Are you mad at me for kissing you last night?" he asked softly. The children were splashing in the pool and having fun and couldn't hear them, and she shook her head.

"No," she replied, smiling shyly at him. "I kissed you too." He felt a thrill at the memory of it and wanted more.

"Do my kids worry you?" he asked, wanting to quell her fears.

"No, I'm falling in love with them." She smiled at him. "I already have. But other things worry me."

"My color?" he asked her, looking her straight in the eyes.

She shook her head. "No, Ash, you're beautiful. I don't care about your color. I just don't want to be sloppy and make a mistake, so someone gets hurt, you or me or the kids. We owe it to them to be careful and responsible, and not just do something because it's easy."

"Relationships are never easy," he said wisely, "and someone always gets hurt, or both, or everyone. You can't give in to fear or let that rule your life." He was a brave man and honored his feelings, and he wanted to respect hers and her fears. He didn't ignore them.

"Have you been in love with a white woman before?" It was an honest question. She knew he had dated them, famous actresses. Claire had been Black like him.

"The answer to that is that my heart is color-blind. I don't care what color a woman is if I love her. I care what color someone is inside, if they're good people or bad. There are some really bad ones out there," he said quietly, and he'd known his share. He was not naïve. But he also knew how profoundly good Oona was.

"I don't think my husband is a bad man. He's confused," Oona said pensively of Charles.

"A lot of people are, and that gets messy, for everyone. If he comes back, would you take him back?" he asked her, and she hesitated.

"I don't know." She wanted to be honest with him too. "I don't think so. He's gone too far by now. He jeopardized our kids, our marriage, his job. He let passion overtake him, and we've all paid the price for it. He's selfish, only thinking of himself. He wants to lead the life he should have figured out thirty years ago. I don't buy that he didn't know, or even suspect. He knew when he met the man he's with now that he was in love with him, and that he's gay. He should have told me then, not a year later when he already had one foot out the door. I'm pissed about that, about his lying to me for a year. Right now he doesn't care about any of us. He just wants to have fun and lead the life he wants, and hold me in reserve in case it doesn't work out in Buenos Aires. That's a little too narcissistic for me," she said. "I can't see myself being with any other man though. I spent all my energy on him, for twenty-five years. I want to be with you, Ash, and your kids, but my emotional piggy bank is empty."

"It didn't seem that way last night when I kissed you. You felt the same things I did," he reminded her, and that was true. She knew she loved him, but she couldn't see a future for them. She was older than he was. And he was a movie star with a big life, much bigger than hers. She couldn't see herself fitting in his world. "I think you're in better shape than you think, and there's more in your emotional bank than you believe. You know what you want, you're just not ready to own it yet." Surprisingly, it was exactly what she did feel. He understood her perfectly, better than she did herself.

"That's true." She wanted to be honest with him.

"Would you go out with me when we go back to the States?" he asked her bluntly. "Or would you be embarrassed?"

"I'd be very, very proud, and afraid every day that some starlet would take you away from me. I can't deal with that, and at my age, that would be inevitable, and I'd get my heart broken. I'm older than you are, Ash. And eight years are a lot." That was one of the major things that worried her, her age and his.

"I don't have a starlet habit," he said, and she smiled.

"That's good to know."

"I did that after Claire and I separated. I was thirty-three years old and gave it up in a year. It was the most boring, tedious year of my life."

"But the starlets were nice to look at, I imagine."

"So is the *Mona Lisa*. I wouldn't want to date her either. She's white too. And that sneaky little smile of hers would annoy the hell out of me. I've never found her beautiful." Oona laughed. But she didn't disagree with him.

"I can't compete with the kind of women you go out with."

"How do you know who I go out with, Oona? You don't know enough about me yet to just cross me off your list or hide from what we're feeling."

"I don't have a list, and I don't want one."

"I'm not going to let you off the hook that easily. You don't meet special people often enough in life to ignore them or waste them when you do. Don't ignore me, Oona." He wanted to kiss her then, but he was afraid one of the kids would look up from their pool games and see them, and it was too soon after their mother's death for them to have to deal with that. He and Oona were both acutely aware of it. They sat quietly then, as she thought about what he had said. She wasn't afraid of his color. She was afraid of getting her heart broken. She wasn't part of his world or as glamorous as the women he dated. She saw herself as a small person with an ordinary life. And his was extraordinary.

When Ashley and the children left at dinnertime, he gave Oona a meaningful look and whispered to her, "Just think about it. Don't waste this. It can work, I know it can." He said it with such strength and certainty for both of them, she almost believed him.

She was haunted by his words all evening after they had gone, and as she got ready for bed. How could he be serious about her? What if it was just a passing fancy because there was no one else around? Loving in the pandemic was like a wartime romance, fraught with uncertainty. But he was a gorgeous man, a movie star, and she was too old for him.

She thought about their color too. She had dated Charles right out of college, and she had never dated anyone of a different race before, or even from a different background. It made no difference as long as they were friends, but a man nearly ten years younger of a different race, what would people think? What would her kids say? She didn't dare ask them. They would be flattered that he found her attractive because he was a movie star, but actually date him? Go out with him? Be in the tabloids with him? She didn't want that, white or Black. She wanted to wake up in the morning next to him and have a normal life with him. But he didn't have a normal life. He was a star.

He made her wish that she was younger. Their age difference bothered her more than his color, and what he would think of her body. Forty-seven didn't look like twenty-five, or even thirty-five. He was stunningly handsome. He made her wish she had paid more attention to her looks. She was in great shape for her age, but Charles was twelve years older than she was, and they made love so seldom that she had stopped caring what she looked like. She had never been vain enough to give herself more than a cursory glance in the mirror, and now suddenly it mattered. And it would matter to others. She was going to be single again, in fact already was, and the thought of having someone other than Charles see the flaws she had ignored and allowed to accumulate was terrifying. She couldn't imagine facing that with a stranger, especially one who looked like Ashley. It was flattering but also horrifying. She lay in bed thinking of him that night, and knew that she couldn't get past the obstacles between them—not just the color, but who he was and how he looked, and the opportunities he had that she could never measure up to. She didn't want to let him go when they left France. But it would be hard to adjust to someone new, or to take the kind of risk it entailed that they'd both be disappointed. It was easier not to love anyone, and just coast into the sunset on her own, even if no one loved her. Love seemed so dangerous to her now, so fraught with risk and possible disappointment. At nearly sixty, Charles had decided that he was gay, had fallen in love with someone else, and their marriage was over. She had had total faith in Charles and their marriage, and he had betrayed her. She realized that if Ashley were white, she would feel no different, and no less scared. Love was a high-stakes game she was afraid to play again.

Charles was older than she was, and Roberto younger than Ashley. She wondered if men didn't think of it that way, or have the same fears. And suddenly she was afraid that she wouldn't be enough for Ashley, after years of thinking that only her mind should matter, not her body. It turned out that that was an illusion. It all mattered, how you looked, how you dressed, how smart or sophisticated you were, how entertaining, how good an athlete, how funny. Married for twenty-five years, she thought you could afford to be forgiving if someone didn't look quite the way they used to or bored you occasionally. And she felt as though she had lost points for all of it and flunked the class entirely. She couldn't risk failing it again and didn't want to with a man who looked like Ashley and was younger. It was easier being alone, and not being vulnerable, than to risk being left again. What would happen when Ashley was sixty-two and still a movie star, and she was an ordinary human at seventy? She cringed at the image. But when she thought of it and closed her eyes, she could hear Ashley in her head and see him in her mind's eye, and knew that she loved him.

Color was not the problem for her. She had never realized that before, but she did now. She didn't want to be with another man who found her unattractive, who didn't bother to make love to her anymore because he said it was too late or too much trouble, or he was tired or had a bad day at the office, or the children might hear them. Suddenly every one of Charles's excuses rang in her head, and she realized that he hadn't found her attractive for years, long before now. And if he had, there would never have been Roberto. Or was Roberto inevitable because of what Charles had been hiding from himself, and from her, since college, and never told her? She didn't want to be left again for someone younger. And with Ashley, it seemed bound to happen. How could it not, even if he didn't see that now?

She fell asleep that night, still turning it around in her mind, and all she knew was that she didn't have the answers, and Ashley was the most beautiful man she'd ever seen, and she wanted him and loved him, but she knew she couldn't have him, or shouldn't, and if she did, she'd regret it. Just as she regretted marrying

Charles now, except for her children. She had wasted twenty-five years with Charles, and she didn't want to make a mistake with Ashley because she loved him. Whether he was Black or white made no difference to her. She was sure of that now, but she was too afraid to move forward. She was sure of that too.

Chapter 9

In spite of Oona's reservations and fears for the future, she and Ashley and his children were together almost every day. He didn't force the issue or crowd her, but he was ever present, and their relationship continued to deepen. She grew more and more attached to his children, and they depended on her in the ways they had their mother. She was a loving female presence in their lives, not trying in any way to replace their mother, but adding a female voice and abilities to their daily lives, with tenderness and discretion.

Simon loved to cuddle on her lap, and Alana turned to her for all the details Ashley couldn't master and didn't try. Questions about hair and clothes, fashion and styles appropriate for Alana that she was eager to try. It was an easy role for Oona, and she loved spending time with them. At the beginning of September, they went to the south of France for a few days, for a change of scene, but Ashley and Oona rapidly agreed that it was too crowded and too risky for the virus, and they went back to Milly-la-Forêt earlier than planned.

Simon and Alana had grown up in England more than they had in L.A., and Ashley's roots and attachment to the Caribbean were strong. It made her realize as she spent time with them that there were subtle differences in how they viewed racial issues. They hadn't grown up with the oppression that had existed in America for years, and the many issues which were still unresolved. Neither Simon nor Alana had ever suffered feelings of discrimination in the schools they went to. Their father had had a happy childhood in Tobago, while their mother had been a little more political, more about feminism than about race, and her long-term boy-friend after Ashley was white, so neither Ashley nor his children made a big issue about Oona being white, nor even thought about it. But being with them made Oona examine her own experiences, growing up in New York. She realized that there had in fact been taboos, but they had been unspoken, never expressed. The taboos were not entirely racial, they were social as well. She had been expected to marry a man from a similar background, but no one had ever openly said he had to be white. It was just assumed he would be if he was from her own social milieu. It was important to her mother that Oona marry a man who had had a good education at a top-notch prep school and college, and she was expected to do the same academically, and apply to the best schools. In Oona's day, staying within the same social and academic boundaries and going to the best universities eliminated, in most cases, men from what was considered "the lower classes," and she had stayed within the range of what was expected of her, without exploring options further afield. She had been neither political nor rebellious growing up, so she had followed the unspoken rules without giving it any further thought. Charles had graduated from Yale, so he was considered by her mother to be an appropriate choice. But underlying those familiar boundaries were the taboos that no one in polite circles voiced, and Oona had paid no attention to them and was unaware of their existence, or at least she didn't spend time thinking about it.

She was expected to have a good job when she graduated from college, and she had, and so had Charles in advertising. Race had never entered into it. And no one ever told her not to date or fall in love with a Black man. Those words were never said. The subject hadn't even come up. One or two of the girls she knew later had married men of a different race, but it had never shocked her or caused comment among her friends. She was friends with people of other races at work. Her own children had never crossed the racial lines in their dating life, but she had never told them not to, nor had Charles, and they had friends of all races. She and Charles had left it up to them. Charles and Oona were liberal in their thinking, but not political about it. What they had conveyed to their children was about human values, not racial ones. Oona had no idea how they would react to Ashley if they knew she was in love with him.

Meghan asked about him from time to time because she knew they were friends, but Oona couldn't imagine them objecting to him, and would have been surprised if they did. Crossing racial lines had never happened in their family, but there was no reason why it shouldn't, or why it would cause them distress. Particularly because he was famous, Ashley fell into a whole other category, as being highly desirable, not someone anyone would object to.

Will was still struggling with the idea that his father was gay, although Meghan seemed to have accepted it. It was more about the shock value and surprise at this late date in their father's life than any prejudice about homosexuality, which they didn't have. Oona couldn't imagine them caring that Ashley and his children were Black.

Oona's main concern was about how different their lives were, and all the inevitable baggage that fame brought with it, and attention from the press, more than about anything to do with race. It simply didn't matter to her, and she didn't care what color Ashley was. But she still couldn't envision herself fitting into the highly public life of a celebrity who had to zealously protect his privacy, and who until now had dated women much younger, more beautiful, and more glamorous than she was. But hearts were unruly and didn't play by the rules or stick to social distinctions. Charles had discovered that when he fell in love with a man, and now Oona was discovering it too. Ashley was deeply embedded in her heart, no matter how much she feared a future with him, and not being up to it, or enough for him.

People recognized Ashley everywhere they went. His children were used to it, but Oona wasn't, and it still startled her when people stopped them for autographs and he graciously signed them, no matter how inconvenient. He was always pleasant and polite, and gracious to his fans.

When they got back to her house and the château after their

brief trip to the south of France, it felt good to be private again and swim in her pool where, more than once, Ashley touched her, when the children weren't watching, or he hoped they weren't. The longer she held back, the more he wanted her, and he confronted her about it one night at the château when the children were asleep upstairs, and he kissed her with all the pent-up passion he felt for her.

"You're driving me insane," he whispered to her after he kissed her, pressing her against him, and she didn't stop him.

"I'm trying to be sensible," she said in a hoarse voice, "so we don't do something we'll both regret."

"Trust me, I won't regret it. I'm a grown-up," he said.

"If we make love, it will change everything, and there's no turning back," although even then, people changed their minds, but not as easily once they'd crossed that line.

"That's what I'm hoping," he said, and she smiled.

"You'll regret it as soon as you get back to L.A. and your real life." She was afraid he would forget her then, or realize she wasn't enough for him. She wasn't young, excessively beautiful, or famous, or even successful in her own career. She didn't even have a job now.

"There's nothing real about my life in L.A. You're real, and I love you. I can't believe I'm saying that, and feeling it for a woman I haven't made love to."

"I'm trying to protect us both," she said earnestly.

"No, you're not. You're scared, of getting hurt, and of shocking your kids. Maybe because I'm younger, or I'm Black. You have a right to a life, Oona."

"That's what their father did. He told them he has a right to happiness. We all do, but not at their expense."

"They're adults, they have a right to make their own mistakes. And we're not a mistake. I've known for four months that this is right, and I'm willing to wait until you figure it out too."

"This isn't a real situation. We're living some kind of war against an unseen enemy, fighting for our lives every day. Your children just lost their mother. Mine have lost their father, or the father they knew. You or I could die any day, like their mother did. How can you build a life on shifting sands in the middle of all that?"

"Because we're the only stable thing we've got, and they've got. This isn't some crazy summer romance, it's the real deal. You're the most stable, sane human being I've ever met, and I have my feet on the ground too. I'm a poor boy from Tobago who got lucky, and if it all goes away, we'll go to Trinidad, or someplace like it, and live simply. I'm not afraid of that, and I don't think you are either. I won't be famous forever."

"You might be." She smiled at him, sure he would be. He was exceptional in every way, and immensely talented. And humble.

"And I might not. But we could be forever, we could grow old together." It was what she had thought about Charles, and it wasn't true. What could she trust now? But he was right, she was afraid that if she reached out to him, he would vanish in thin air, and she would be alone again, with a broken heart, worse than when Charles left her. She had never loved Charles as she did Ash, even without having made love. She didn't need to have sex with him to know she loved him, although she dreamt of him at night.

A few days after they got back from the south of France, in early

September, he got a call from his agent in L.A. The series in England had definitely been canceled, and they wanted him for a series in L.A., with all the necessary precautions for Covid. His agent said he had to take it, it was an opportunity that would never come again, with a star-studded cast, and Ashley was going to be one of the stars. Another actor had been given the role and had just dropped out for health reasons. The producers were desperate for Ash, and they were offering him a fortune for the part. And realistically, as he said to Oona, he needed the money. He couldn't stay out of work forever. He had to go back. He slept on it, and accepted it the next day. He had to be back in L.A. in a week, in order to quarantine for two weeks before they started preproduction. The money for the production was already set and in place, and his part was the last left to fill. They'd had trouble finding the right actor for it and Ashley was the perfect fit.

He told Oona after he called his agent and accepted the role. He didn't want to leave France, but he had no choice. It was a job he had to take.

"Will you come to see us in L.A. when you come back to the States?" he asked her. She nodded but didn't look sure. Ashley was worried. He didn't want to lose her now, but he had to work.

"I have to find a job too," she reminded him, but the headhunters were telling her that there were none like the job she'd had, and houses like hers had gone out of style, which was why Hargrove had closed her imprint. Purely highbrow literary work just wasn't financially viable. She'd have to take a pay cut and start at the bottom in commercial fiction, which was discouraging.

She had decided to file for divorce when she went back. Charles

169

had been in Argentina for eight months by then, and the marriage was over for Oona. She realized now that it had been over years before he left her, and she had to face it. Charles knew it too, although she hadn't told him about the divorce yet.

Oona was at the château for dinner with Ashley and the kids the night he had accepted the starring role in the series they would be shooting in L.A. He was serious and quiet at dinner. It had been a big decision for him, although it was an amazing part. He didn't feel ready to leave his safe little world in France at the château, and more than anything he didn't want to leave Oona. Simon and Alana had begun to calm down after their mother's death. They were still sad about it, and always would be, but the stability of the life he was providing for them with Oona's help had had a positive effect on them. Simon was no longer having nightmares, and Alana had gotten very attached to Oona, and now he had to uproot them again. Both children looked shocked when he told them they were leaving in a week.

"Is Oona coming with us?" Alana asked him, and she and Ashley exchanged a look before he answered.

"Not right away," he answered, and Oona stepped in.

"I'm going to stay here for a while and see how things are going in the States. And you're all going to be busy in L.A."

"I don't want to go to school there," Simon said, scowling at his father, and then he turned a pleading look to Oona. "I want you to come," he said to her.

"I'll come and visit you when I get back, but I need to do some things here." In truth, there was nothing she needed to do there, but she had nothing to do in New York, and she was happier in

France, although it wouldn't be the same without them. They had formed their own little family unit all summer. She didn't want Ashley to leave either, but she understood how important the part was for his career, better than the children did.

"Will we have a babysitter?" Alana asked her father, and he nodded.

"I'm going to be working, and I can't leave you alone. They have some very complicated setup for Covid on the set, with revolving schedules and the cast working on different shifts. If I understand it correctly, we'll be working two weeks on and one week off, with testing and some kind of short quarantine in between. It's going to cost them a fortune in extra time the way they're doing it, but they don't want anyone in the cast or crew to get sick." Alana had made a face as soon as he had said he was hiring a sitter.

"We want Oona, not a babysitter," Simon said, and stopped eating his dinner.

"Oona will come and see us when she can, and we'll be together," he tried to reassure them.

"Yeah, when you're not working or in quarantine," Alana said with a glum look. They went upstairs to their rooms afterward, and Ashley and Oona stayed at the table to talk about his plans again.

"We're all going to miss you," he said, as sad as his children to be leaving her.

"It was bound to happen," Oona said. He had been there for six months, and the entertainment industry was trying to get things rolling again. He'd been offered a fabulous part in the series.

"Do you have any idea when you'll come back to the States?" he asked her. Until that day, neither of them had felt ready to leave. The Covid numbers of new cases were still high all over the U.S., and it still seemed safer in France.

"I'll start working on it. I want to see some headhunters, and I need to see my lawyer for the divorce. I haven't told Charles I've made the decision yet. I haven't heard from him since July, and I want to tell him before his lawyer gets served with papers." It seemed only fair, although he hadn't been fair with her. Oona wanted to do it right and not start a war with him.

"And then you'll come to L.A.?" He was pressing her, dreading leaving her, particularly with nothing set between them. She fully expected him to come to his senses when he left and forget her.

"I'll stop and see Will on the way. I talked to Meghan the other day, and she wants to stay in Kenya for her full term, until February. The numbers were very low in Africa, so she's safer there than anywhere else, although I hate not seeing her for all this time. She's thinking of signing up for another year, but I want her to come home for a visit before she does. It's been too long."

Ashley had hoped he'd have more time with Oona before they had to leave. He was so happy with her and so were his kids. They had lost their mother and he didn't want them to lose Oona too. And she was cognizant of it as well. She didn't want to lose Ashley and the children either. And as long as they were together, she didn't have to make any big decisions. Now everything was going to change.

"It won't be the same here without you," she said softly, and he reached across the table and held her hand. They hadn't come to any conclusions about the relationship. He was still trying to convince her that it could work, even long-term. And so far she had refused to commit. It was hard to trust love again, particularly with the challenges they would face.

They sat in his garden that night, holding hands, talking about his plans. The cast he would be working with was dazzling, and it underlined what she had said about his being a star. They were some of the biggest names in Hollywood. A number of them were film actors who had never done TV before. It was going to be a star-studded production, and he would be one of the biggest stars of all.

"They won't even let me bring the kids on the set because of Covid. I'm going to be away from them a lot with the rolling schedule and quarantine. If someone gets sick, they don't want to lose the whole cast, so we'll have alternating groups. It's going to make the shooting schedule a nightmare. But you can call me whenever you want." As he said it, Oona felt an ache in her heart. She suddenly realized how painful it would be not to see him every day, or the children, not to have meals with them, or go on adventures, or to *brocantes* with Ashley. In spite of the menace of the virus, they had been extremely close for four months, and had a very comfortable, cozy life together. There would be no more visits to historical châteaux with them, no more long nighttime conversations with Ashley. She was thinking of all the things she would miss without them, and turned to look at Ashley with a lump in her throat.

"This is really hard," she said in a choked voice, as he held her hand and nodded. This was exactly what she had wanted to avoid. She hadn't wanted to get too attached to them, and to him, and she had anyway. It had snuck up on all four of them. Whether legitimate or not, they had formed a family unit and were deeply attached to each other. Oona and Ashley both knew it, and it was too late now to detach. He just wanted to enjoy these final days together before he and the children left. It was too late now to dissolve the bonds painlessly. They would each lose a piece of their heart to the others when they left. A major piece in the case of Ashley and Oona. Her plan not to get too deeply involved with them hadn't worked. She had forgotten all the rules of detachment herself. She had maintained no boundaries with the kids, and even fewer with him. He would have given anything to have her go to L.A. with them, but he knew how adamant she was, and how afraid. And there was no time left to prove to her it could work.

"We'll just have to make the best of it," he said as they sat in the garden chairs, and he leaned over and kissed her. They kissed a lot these days, but had gone no further, for fear of where it would lead. Oona didn't trust either of them to keep things in check. They wanted each other too desperately to listen to reason, and their hearts won the argument that night, faced with the reality of Ashley leaving in a week. They quietly went upstairs to the unused bedrooms on an upper floor, and she followed him willingly. They opened one of the rooms and locked the door behind them, and she undressed him as he undressed her, in the heat of passion and the fear of loss. Their clothes fell in a heap on the floor, their bodies entwined as he had wanted for months, and all her caution and objections disappeared in the moment as love took over. They were both breathless and clung to each other afterward. And then he looked down at her, worried.

"Oh my God, Oona, I'm sorry, are you angry at me?" She smiled and shook her head, lying back against the pillows, loving him as never before.

"I love you, Ash. I'm sorry it took me so long to get here. I've wanted you from the beginning. Maybe that's why I was afraid to let it happen, I knew that once I did, you'd own me forever. It was stupid of me to wait so long, knowing how much I love you."

"You're not sorry?" He looked at her with relief and sat on the bed next to her.

"No, I'm not," she said, and kissed him passionately, and he pulled away and smiled.

"Then let's do it again," he said, laughing, and began making love to her for the second time, and they forgot everything but each other.

They stayed upstairs in their secret bedroom for a long time, talking and whispering, and kissing and discovering each other's bodies, and afterward they took a shower and dressed and went back downstairs feeling closer than ever before. An important barrier had been crossed.

"I wish you could spend the night," he whispered to her when he walked her to the front hall full of ancestral portraits. They had been together for hours, making up for lost time. "Simon's in my bed," he said regretfully. He would have loved to spend the night with her.

"It was wonderful . . . perfect . . ." she said, and put a fingertip on his lips to silence him, and then kissed him again. She was everything he had dreamt of and more. She had a beautiful body, and more than that she was a wonderful person and he loved her. And she knew for certain that she loved him. It was what he had wanted to happen for months and what she was so afraid of. Now that he was leaving, she wanted to face her fears, and commit herself to him fully before they parted.

She was wearing the jeans and pink sweater she had arrived in. She had no makeup on, and her red hair was loose down her back nearly to her waist. She put her pink ballet flats on and he walked her to her car. He would have driven her home, but he couldn't leave the children. It had been an unforgettable night. They could hear the birds chirping just before the dawn.

"Thank you," he whispered to her, and kissed her, leaning through the car window. "I'll come for breakfast tomorrow, as soon as the housekeeper gets here." She nodded and started the car, waving as she drove across the drawbridge over the moat, and then she was gone, and he walked back into the château, with a smile on his face and a bright light in his heart.

Chapter 10

When Ashley arrived at La Belle Florence the next morning, Marie, the housekeeper, had just arrived. She was tidying the kitchen, and Ashley waved as he rushed past and raced up the stairs. Marie didn't try to stop him. He was a regular fixture, and she was sure he was welcome upstairs in Oona's room. They seemed very much in love to her.

He opened the door silently, closed it behind him, and tiptoed into the room. Oona was still sound asleep, naked under the sheets, as he took off his clothes and slipped gently into the bed beside her, admiring her beautiful face as she slept. And then, sensing him, she opened an eye and smiled, and he kissed her, and she put her arms around him, and they made love again. It was as passionate as the night before, and infinitely tender, and she lay in his arms afterward, at peace, as he rolled onto his back next to her, with a sated smile and a blissful expression. Making love to her was as wonderful as he had thought it would be. She had touched him to his very soul the night before and had just done it again.

"Did Marie let you in?" she asked him, lying on her back, and he grinned.

"She had the front door open, and she was in the kitchen. I think she had just let Florence out. I was in a hurry to come upstairs." He smiled at her, and propped himself up on one elbow, to admire her more closely. "I may have destroyed your reputation," he said sheepishly, and she laughed.

"I don't think she'll be surprised. You're here all the time. And she likes you." He had signed autographs for both of Marie's sisters and a cousin. "What are we doing today?" she asked him, and stretched, and he leaned down to kiss her.

"There's a *brocante* I thought we could go to. It's going to be so strange being back in the States, without you," he said, momentarily sad again.

"It will be sad here too," she said, and sat up in bed, admiring him, as he got out of bed and walked around her room naked, admiring small antique objects and some rose quartz obelisks that belonged to the owners, and photographs of her children she'd put on the mantel. He had a spectacular body, toned to perfection. She put a robe on and came up behind him and put her arms around him, and he looked over his shoulder at her and smiled.

"I'm giving you fair warning, Oona Kelly," he said. She had decided over the summer to go back to her maiden name, once she had made the decision to get divorced. "If you don't come to L.A. soon, I'm breaking their quarantine, and coming to New York to kidnap you. Just so you know what will happen if you don't come to California soon."

"I promise I will, as soon as I get things taken care of in New York. I want to look at the house in East Hampton too. I think Charles and I should either sell it and split the money, or rent it out. Half of New York has moved to the Hamptons because of Covid. We could probably get a good rent for it, if Charles is willing. I don't know if he wants to use it or not. I asked him, but he hasn't answered."

They shared a shower then, dressed for the *brocante,* went downstairs, and made breakfast. Ashley had a hearty appetite after the night's exertions, and Oona had coffee and a slice of toast, as usual. Florence appeared when they sat down at the breakfast table, and begged Ashley for something to eat since he could never resist her and always gave her a treat.

"You're bringing Florence home, aren't you?" he asked her, as she set a plate of fried eggs in front of him.

"Of course." She had fallen in love with her little rescue dog. All her curly fur had come back in the bald patches, and her coat was thicker than ever. She looked healthy and a little rounder than when she arrived. Marie always spoiled her with extra portions and she looked like a little curly white ball now. "I'll bring her to California with me. I don't want to leave her in New York." New York still seemed so far away and her life there, and the people in it, so unreal, like the distant past. She'd had emails from some of her colleagues at work. It sounded like everyone she knew had fled from the city to the country, to stay with their parents or at their own weekend homes. The city was said to be a ghost town, and crime had increased on the streets, with robberies, muggings, and looting. Some of the luxury stores in Soho had been robbed repeatedly. Gail had told her that it was scary being a woman out alone at night now. And Ashley said he'd heard the same about L.A. People were hungry, angry, and out of work. And in California, they were letting looters and petty thieves have open season, stealing whatever they wanted. No one was going to argue with them, not even the police, since many of the looters were armed.

When Ashley and Oona finished breakfast, they went back to the château. The children were just waking up, and he made pancakes for them. Simon sat on Oona's lap while he waited for his breakfast. He was wearing his pajamas, and Alana arrived at the table in jeans and a Minnie Mouse T-shirt and red sandals. She looked adorable and had her father's knack for looking stylish whatever she wore. Ashley told them about the *brocante* and they agreed to go if they could swim when they got back, and Ashley and Oona agreed. It was an easy negotiation.

They took off for a neighboring village later that morning, and the kids followed them around the *brocante*, bored with the vintage and antique objects that fascinated their father and Oona. Ashley had spent half an hour going over eighteenth-century miniatures painted on ivory, many of them of the members of the court of Louis XVI, while Oona had fun at a stand with vintage hats and bought two, one of them a very chic black hat from World War II made in Paris, and a beautiful romantic straw hat from the nineteenth century, with pale blue satin ribbons. She looked wonderful in hats, and Ashley took pictures of her with his phone.

"Did you buy something?" Oona asked him when she saw he was carrying a small package.

"A miniature of a general from Louis the Sixteenth's army. I thought it would be fun to have," he said nonchalantly. And he had bought a pair of very handsome dueling pistols that were purely decorative and no longer worked, and Oona was carrying her hats. They left after an hour when the kids complained that they were bored, went back to La Belle Florence to swim, and spent a lazy day at the pool, and then Alana and Simon watched a movie in her theater, while Oona and their father sat in the living room and talked.

They spent as much time together as they could that week, doing all the things they most enjoyed. There was a feeling of fleeting moments as the time sped by. Both Oona and Ashley were acutely aware that their time together was running out, and there was a bittersweet tenderness to it. The kids caught them kissing several times, and Simon guffawed when he saw them, and asked Oona the question again that he had asked in the beginning when he arrived.

"Are you my dad's girlfriend now since you kissed him?"

"Yeah, Simon," she responded with a smile, "I guess I am." He seemed satisfied with the answer, and Alana gave a knowing smile. They both liked the idea, and Ashley looked pleased when she said it.

"So will you come to L.A. with us now?" Simon asked her with a pleading look.

"I'll come soon, I promise. I have some things I have to do in New York." He liked the first answer better than the second.

Whenever they were sure that the children were asleep, or out riding with the stable hands, they found a place and time to make love, in the pool cabana and once in her bedroom with the door locked.

The days went by too quickly, and Oona had a rising sense of panic as the day for their departure approached. Ashley had a feeling of dread about leaving her, particularly after Claire's death nearly three months before. But Oona was in good health and didn't have Claire's pathology, which had made her high risk and more vulnerable to the virus. He kept urging Oona to be careful after they left. He didn't like the idea of leaving her alone in France, although she had been there for three months before she met him and had gone through the first lockdown alone. There was talk of another one coming as the numbers began to rise through September. As the weather began to cool, the second spike of the virus rose to alarming heights, and confinement seemed inevitable. Ashley and the children were leaving in time, and Oona began to plan her own departure.

She had rented the house until October, with the possibility of extending it if she wished to. After staying for so long, she had begun paying a nominal rent again for the house that summer. The owners had been very generous with her, and she didn't want to take undue advantage of it. They said they were grateful that the house was occupied, and all the reports they'd had indicated that she was an exceptional tenant, so they were grateful she had stayed, and she to be there in the house she'd come to love. She knew she would always be grateful for the time she'd spent there, and the relationship with Ashley that had begun there.

He was planning to return whenever possible to stay at the château again, and he hoped that next time Oona would stay there with him, if they came alone, or had been together for longer so as not to shock his children. He even liked the idea of renting La Belle Florence if it was available. They both loved it and had a strong sentimental tie to it now.

Simon and Alana seemed very comfortable with their father's blossoming relationship with Oona, but it still seemed too soon after their mother's death for Oona to stay with him openly now, and Oona particularly wanted to remain circumspect around his children. They were very young, and Ashley had never had women stay with him when they were around. He and Oona were in agreement on that. She had made the adjustment well from friend to lover, and was thriving on the love they shared and were able to give full expression to now. It hadn't hurt their friendship, and had only deepened it, and they were closer than ever.

On their last night, she helped the children pack and close their bags. Ashley had packed all the treasures and mementos he had purchased at various *brocantes,* and the children had a few as well. Ashley and Oona shepherded the children into bed early, since they had to get up before dawn to leave the château at six-thirty A.M. to check in for their ten A.M. flight to L.A. There were two Air France flights a week to Los Angeles, and they were flying almost empty with Americans, spouses of Americans, and permanent resident foreign green card holders returning to the States. It was never enough to fill the plane, but enough to continue to fly the route from Charles de Gaulle airport. The children knew they would have to wear masks for the entire eleven-hour trip. Oona had bought children's masks for them. Simon's had Mickey Mouse on them and Alana's were rainbow colored.

They were asleep when Ashley checked at nine-thirty, and he and Oona went quietly to their favorite guest room on the upper floor, which had become their secret love nest since they had become lovers. Ashley lit a candle and they made love by candlelight, with the moonlight shining through the windows. Oona looked beautiful in the soft light, and they couldn't get enough of each other. Ashley wanted to take her with him. He was desperately afraid that he would never see her again, that either she wouldn't come home or something untoward would happen to her, and he'd be too far away to help her.

"Promise me that you'll be careful—the numbers are getting worse." But they were even worse now in New York and she was planning to go back. The world was fraught with dangers now, for all of them, even Simon and Alana. Children got the virus too.

"You too," she reminded him.

"The set we'll be working on sounds like a hospital the way it's run," he reassured her, and then they made love in the moonlight again. Oona had blown out the candle—they didn't need it—and they were still awake before the dawn when they had to wake the children. They were going to tell the children she had come early, so she could spend the last hours with him. She'd asked Marie to feed the dog before she left and when she arrived the next morning. Marie knew what that meant and promised to take care of it. Oona knew that Florence would sleep on her bed and be safe at home. There were too many places for her to get lost at the château.

Ashley kissed Oona for a last time before they left the room. "Don't forget how much I love you," he said to Oona. "Don't forget this," and there was no way she could. It seemed like a miracle to both of them that they had found each other.

He went to wake the children then, and she waited for him downstairs in the kitchen, and started making breakfast for them. It was ready by the time they came down. Simon looked sleepy-eyed, and yawned, and Alana looked tidy in her traveling clothes. The children ate quickly and went upstairs to brush their teeth, and after they left the kitchen, Ashley put a small package in her hands. He was smiling when he handed it to her and looked pleased with himself. He had meant to give it to her the night before and had forgotten in their shared passion, which took precedence.

She kissed him even before she unwrapped it and thanked him, and he gave her a lingering kiss and then waited for her to open it. They had wrapped it at the *brocante* in a piece of bubble wrap and gift paper, and as she carefully undid it, she found herself looking at a delicately painted oval miniature on ivory of a beautiful young girl with blond curls peeking out from under a pink silk bonnet, with a little dog in her arms who looked like a distant relative of Oona's Florence. The pretty young girl was smiling and looked directly into one's eyes as one looked at her.

"Oh, she's lovely, Ash. She's so pretty—did they know who she is?" It didn't really matter. She had so much charm and spirit she almost seemed alive as they gazed at her, as Oona carefully held the miniature that was about the size of the palm of her hand, in a delicate gold frame.

"It's Florence de Montmarrin," Ashley said victoriously, "the great love of the last king of France, whom the house is named after, and her little dog looks a lot like your Florence. I was drawn to it immediately at the miniature stand at the *brocante* the other day, and I couldn't believe it when they said who it was. You were meant to have it, Oona. You can see why the king loved her—she jumps right out at you, doesn't she?" Oona had tears in her eyes as she looked at her and then at Ash.

"It's the most beautiful gift I've ever gotten," she said, unable to stop looking at the girl. She looked as though she was about to speak to them. "And her little dog looks just like Flo, that's so odd, isn't it? Thank you, Ash, I love her. I'm going to put her somewhere very special. I think she's the godmother of our relationship," Oona said in a tone of awe, for him, and the priceless gift he had given her. She wrapped the delicate miniature up again carefully, and kissed Ashley again, just as the children came back into the room. It was almost time to go. They were excited about the trip, although they were sad to leave Oona and the château.

"We'll come back here again one day," Ashley said in a serious tone, "and we'll remember the good times we had here too." He looked at Oona as he said it and she nodded, and a minute later the car arrived, and she sent the children to the bathroom before the trip and went to check their rooms to make sure they hadn't forgotten anything, while Ashley did the same in his own room. When they met on the stairs on the way down, Oona was carrying a small, bedraggled brown teddy bear she'd found in Simon's bed and Ashley rolled his eyes.

"Oh, Lord, you found Mr. Bear—Simon would have been devastated if we forgot him. You just saved the day and the entire trip." Oona handed the little bear to Ashley, and he tucked him into the travel bag he had slung over his shoulder. Ashley was wearing a black leather jacket, a black T-shirt, black jeans, and cowboy boots. He looked every inch the star he was. He had a certain air about him that attracted attention immediately and told you he was someone special. He put dark glasses on, which instantly made him look even more like a movie star, and Oona smiled.

"You look amazing," she said to him, and he grinned with the whitest, widest smile in the world. There was no hiding who he was, and he didn't try to. He straightened Simon's jacket and tucked in his shirt. Both children were wearing jeans and their Euro Disney T-shirts and running shoes. And they each had a bag of things to do on the plane. Ashley told Simon he had Mr. Bear safely tucked into his own bag.

"Oona found him in your bed," he told the boy, and Simon looked at her with huge brown eyes of gratitude.

"Thank you, Oona," he said.

"He didn't want to miss the trip," she told him.

They left the château, piled into the van Ashley had arranged, and set off on the trip to the airport. They were right on schedule. Oona and Ashley sat in the row behind the driver, with the children behind them. The drive went smoothly, and Simon fell asleep. Alana played a game on her iPad, and Oona and Ashley held hands for most of the trip. She felt peaceful sitting next to him, and wished she was going with him, but she still had a few more weeks in her time there, before she went back to the States too. She didn't know yet when she would be going to California, but she hoped it would be soon. She had to work out the dates with Will too.

They checked their bags at the airport, but Oona couldn't go into the terminal at Roissy with the new Covid rules. They lingered on the sidewalk for a little while and then a member of the ground crew came to get them. They were all wearing their masks, and Oona had packed extras for them for the trip. Mickey Mouse for Simon, the rainbow one for Alana, and Ashley was wearing a black mask he always wore. He pulled Oona aside when the moment came to enter the terminal, held her in his powerful arms, and looked into her eyes, and everything he felt for her was in the way he looked at her. He took off his mask and hers and kissed her.

"Remember how much I love you," he whispered. "I'll be waiting for you, Oona. Come soon."

"I love you, Ash," she whispered. "Thank you for everything, and the beautiful little portrait of Florence."

"Just take care of you, and get home safely. I'll call you when we land," he promised, and they put their masks on and walked back to the children.

"Ready to rock and roll?" he asked them, and Simon nodded, then wrapped his arms around Oona's waist and squeezed her tight.

"I love you, Oonie," he said, with his face buried in her sweater, and his voice muffled.

"I love you too, Simon," she said, fighting back tears, and kissed the top of his head, and then she hugged Alana. "Call me whenever you want," she reminded her. "Nail polish consultations at any hour." She had given her three shades of pink polish for her toes.

Ashley squeezed her hand and hugged her one last time, with his mask on, and led the children away, into the terminal. He turned back in the doorway and their eyes met, and he touched his heart, and she touched hers, and then they were gone. She watched them through the glass door until they disappeared into the terminal, and what she had feared would happen already had—he had left with her heart, just as she knew he would, but it didn't seem so scary after all. And he had left his with her.

The driver took her back to Milly-la-Forêt and the trip seemed longer on the way back. Oona looked out the window and thought about Ashley and the children. And as they drove up the driveway to La Belle Florence, she looked at her watch, and it was the exact moment they would be taking off if they left on time. She heard a ping on her cell phone that indicated she had a text, and looked at it. It was from Ashley, and a big red heart appeared, flying into the sky. She smiled and put her phone back into her pocket, praying for their safety, walked into the house, and went to look at the beautiful miniature he had given her. That she was alone again hit her like a wrecking ball as soon as she walked into the house. But somewhere in the sky over Paris was a man she loved, and who loved her. And one day, if all went well, she would see him again.

The portrait of Florence de Montmarrin looked at her from her hand, smiling and full of joy as she held her little dog. She looked to be about eighteen in the delicate painting. She was a woman who had been passionately loved by a king. Oona could feel her spirit around her like a blessing on her union with Ashley, and a promise that they would be together again.

Chapter 11

The silence at La Belle Florence was deafening when Oona got home from the airport, and she had no plans that day. She had no one to make lunch for, and no one to have dinner with, and there was no one in the pool squealing and having fun. She sat in a lounge chair and tried to read in the September sunshine, but couldn't concentrate. She kept thinking about Ashley, Alana, and Simon on the plane, and hoped they were all right. They were traveling first class, and Oona knew they would have VIP service to get them through customs and immigration in L.A.

She missed them terribly, but she still felt that she was in the right place and even as much as she had come to love Ashley and opened her heart to him, she had a bond to France and the house now that she wasn't ready to give up. She was planning to go home, but she hadn't chosen a date yet. He was going to be sequestered while filming the new series, according to the Covid rules, so she couldn't see him anyway. He was planning to hire a nanny to be with his children as soon as he got home, and he had to quarantine for ten days, get Covid tested, and report for work at the location where they'd be staying. He would have to live on the set with the other actors and the crew, being tested regularly. He would be given occasional breaks every third week, when he could see the kids, and would then have to be tested again afterward. Oona just hoped that the nanny would be good, and she was sorry not to be with them. But she had to take care of her own business first.

The Covid numbers had been rising noticeably in France since the end of August. All the traveling around Europe during the summer and the crowded vacation spots in the south of France, particularly in Saint-Tropez, had taken a toll on the country's recovery—the virus was slipping rapidly out of control again, and another confinement seemed almost inevitable.

Ashley called her at ten forty-five that night, after they had landed and cleared immigration. They had needed no test to reenter the United States from Europe, and quarantine was suggested but not mandatory. The plane had been half full, and with the help of VIP ground crew, Ashley and the children were whisked through the formalities and escorted to the van waiting for them. He called Oona from the sidewalk before he got in the van, while they were loading the luggage. Simon and Alana had slept on the long flight and were wide awake once they landed. They wanted to buy food at one of the airport restaurants and they were surprised to see that they were all closed, and LAX looked like an empty movie set of an airport. There were hardly any people there. Many flights had been canceled and most people were afraid of the risks of travel. There were no tourists.

Ash had thought of Oona for the entire flight, whenever he was awake, which was most of the time. Covid measures on the plane were strict, and the fourth seat in first class had been empty, so they had all of first class to themselves, which from a health standpoint was reassuring. Everyone they saw, in the plane and on the ground, wore masks. Many people took them off once they stepped outside the terminal, but until that point, Ashley had felt relatively safe, and the crew kept reassuring the passengers throughout the flight that the air filter systems were a new design and the air was pure. Ashley hoped they were right. He was surprised to see how many people outside the terminal weren't wearing masks. In France everyone was wearing them, but there was more of a feeling of freedom in the States. He hadn't been back since the pandemic began, and it was strange to see the difference between Europe and the States. People seemed to follow fewer rules in the United States.

He called Oona from the sidewalk, standing in the California sun, feeling like he had landed on another planet. He smiled as soon as she answered the phone. She sounded happy to hear from him. She was reading in bed when he called and said she missed them. They talked for a few minutes, and he promised to call her from the house. On the way home, there were people on the streets but not as many as usual.

The van the studio had arranged for him took him to his home in Bel Air. It was a sprawling modern house on one level, with rooms for Alana and Simon at the opposite end of the house from the master suite. There was another bedroom for guests, Ashley's home office, a gym with state-of-the-art equipment, a kitchen and dining room, an enormous living room with a view of the garden, and a pool. It didn't have warmth or charm, but it had everything he needed. It had been done by a decorator, and the antique treasures he liked to find looked slightly out of place in the stark modern décor. But they added an eclectic feeling and some personality.

The housekeeper had stocked the fridge with kid-friendly food and salads and fresh produce for him. There were several fancy catered meals in the freezer along with pizzas, which the kids would like, and everything was immaculate.

The driver set their bags down in their respective rooms, and once he was sure that the kids were okay, Ashley sat down on his bed and called Oona again. It was almost midnight for her by then, and three o'clock in the afternoon in L.A.

"I feel like I've landed in another galaxy," he said to her in a warm tone. "It doesn't feel like home anymore. I want to be back at La Belle Florence with you." Everything around him looked sterile and unfamiliar, and he felt as though he was seeing it with new eyes. And it felt to her like he was in another universe too.

Every fiber of his being was crying out for her, and he longed to be back in France, where everything seemed familiar now, and on a more human scale, and real, like Oona. He knew his life was going to get even more different when he got back to work. He had to do an obligatory quarantine now for ten days, at his home, get tested, and then report to start filming the series.

"Were the kids okay on the flight?" Oona asked him, and he

closed his eyes, listening to her voice. She sounded tired but happy to hear from him, and she said she missed him too.

"They were really good. There are no fancy meals even in first class now—it's all been restricted because of Covid. Everything is different now. And I forget how different everything is from Europe until I get here. I always feel out of place here, especially now after six months at the château and visiting you at your place. There's nothing old here, and no charm." He said how much he missed her.

"I miss you too," Oona said, and he thought she sounded sad. "It's not the same without you here." She was so used to seeing him all the time now, and the children for the past two months. Even the dog had seemed unusually quiet all day, stayed close to her, and slept in the sun. Florence had looked disappointed when Oona came home alone, as though she expected to see Ashley and the children.

"I have to start interviewing nannies for the kids tomorrow, and be in quarantine for the next ten days. It'll give me time to study the scripts." He was back in his familiar world now, in a life she had never seen and couldn't even imagine. It made him seem even farther away as she listened to him.

"I hope you find a nanny they like."

"They don't want any nanny. They want to be with us," he said simply. "But since I have to live on the set part of the time, I need someone staying here with them." It was what he had been afraid of when their mother died. Having them with him in L.A. while he was working was going to be a hard juggling act he wasn't prepared for, but he didn't want to send them to his sister in

Trinidad—he had to make it work so they could stay with him. "I wish you were here," he said to Oona. "It's going to be lonely in bed tonight." It seemed impossible to believe that twenty-four hours ago they had made love in the moonlight at the château, and now they were six thousand miles apart, and it felt like it. He felt like a stranger in his own house. He had bought it after the divorce, but it had never felt like home to him. He didn't even like the art the decorator had picked for him, and wondered if Oona would like it. He suddenly looked at the place with different eyes, wondering how Oona would feel about it. He wished now that it was cozier and more inviting. Everything had hard edges and sharp lines.

He went to check on the kids after he talked to Oona. They had helped themselves to food from the fridge and looked half asleep at the kitchen table. He sat with them for a few minutes and then went to check his messages and emails and discovered that there was a mountain of scripts on his desk to study. He would have plenty to do for the next ten days. The role he had in the series was demanding, and he needed time to study it. He was even going to do his own stunt work. They had taken out additional insurance so he could. He had to fill out forms to get the kids into school. They'd need help with the assignments online and with the homework. Claire had always worked on homework with them, but he didn't have the time. He would have to explain that to the nanny he hired, along with everything else he had to do the next day.

By the time he went to check on the kids again, they were both sound asleep on their beds in their travel clothes. He smiled as he looked at them and decided to let them sleep. Coming to L.A. was going to be a big adjustment for them.

He went back to his office then, and answered as many emails as he could. By the time he finished, he was feeling lonely, sad, and overwhelmed. It was hard coming home, starting a series, and being solely responsible for two children. He felt like he was about to climb Mount Everest.

When Oona hung up, she lay in bed, thinking about Ashley and missing him. He seemed so far away now, and he had sounded stressed on the phone, with everything he had to do, and there was very little she could help him with long distance. He needed someone there in L.A.

It was only a short jump from there to open the floodgates to the inner voices that tormented her, about how ill-prepared she was for his life, how ill-suited to it, and inadequate. It was all so simple when they were in France, just the four of them. He wasn't working, and there were no reporters hounding them, miraculously, since people in the area knew he was there and it wasn't a secret. But people had other things to think about for the moment with the pandemic, so Ashley and Oona had gotten a break and could move around like normal people. Now he was going to be filming what was expected to be one of the biggest shows on TV. He would be a hot press item, and on social media for a very long time. How did she think the relationship would survive with a major show and TV stardom? He was younger, he was famous, and she had no idea how to deal with it. The voices of fear told her that she would fall flat on her face and blow it. She had nothing to compare it to, and no preparation for his life, and in no time she would be an embarrassment to him. There were no significant publishing houses in L.A. where she could get a job if she stayed with him, and she would be completely dependent on him to make their life in L.A. work.

By the time she fell asleep, she had totally panicked herself, and convinced herself that she wasn't up to being the right partner for him, and would embarrass him, due to her age, her look, and the very different life she had led. She had been an editor and a wife for her entire career, not a movie star's girlfriend. She had no idea what to do on the red carpet, and didn't have the right wardrobe for it, or the looks, she told herself. And she was sure that the media would be horrified at the eight years between them. Ashley wasn't there to reassure her, and tell her it would be fine, and he'd rather be with her than any other woman on the planet. He meant it each time he said it to her. But six thousand miles away, in Milly-la-Forêt, she no longer believed him. The voices of her deeply embedded fears were more convincing.

She wondered if it was a good idea to go to L.A., or if she should end it now before she went through the humiliation of failing when she got there and losing his respect for her. She fell into a deeply troubled sleep and had nightmares almost immediately. She and Ashley were on the red carpet at a premiere and reporters and paparazzi were shoving microphones into her face and filming her, when her dress tore away and she was standing naked in front of them, and Ashley told her to leave immediately and said he never wanted to see her again, and a new very young, beautiful girl took her place. Her dream seemed all too real, and much too likely. She had a fitful night, while Ashley lay on his bed in L.A.

fantasizing about her, and wishing he were back in France with her. He hoped she'd come back to the States soon, but he knew she was having trouble leaving France. She felt safe and comfortable in the beautiful house. She was afraid of the violence of the virus in the States, and the street violence as well, which was rampant in the United States, along with people not wearing masks and being careless about preventive measures that were commonplace in Europe and had been for months.

She called Gail to talk about it the next day.

"Tell me the truth," she said to her old friend. "How bad is the virus in the States? Some people say it's nothing and totally manageable. Others say it's the end of the world."

"We've all learned to live with it. If you're careful, you should be okay."

"I'm living outside a village smaller than Central Park. I see only the housekeeper every day, and the gardeners at a distance outdoors. If I want to see a friend, I can meet her for breakfast, at a respectful, safe distance. People seem much less careful about the virus in New York."

"That's probably true," Gail said. "It varies from city to city and state to state. Politics got into it somehow, and whether or not you wear a mask depends on what political party you belong to."

"That makes no sense," Oona said.

"No, it doesn't," Gail agreed. "Why? Are you thinking about coming back?" Gail asked her. "Your kids aren't even here."

"I need to straighten my life out at some point. I want to file for divorce. I have an apartment there, and the country house—I need to figure out what to keep and what we should sell. I need to find a new job. And Ashley went back to L.A. He wants me to come and see them, and I can't stay in a rented house here forever. It's beginning to feel like time to go home, although in some ways it's more comfortable here, and feels safer Covid-wise."

"Does Ashley want you to stay in L.A. with him?"

"Maybe. Probably. I don't see how I'd fit into his life. He's a star. He's dated half the actresses in Hollywood. I don't see myself in that picture. I need to find a job in New York and figure out what Charles and I are going to do."

"I thought he did figure it out when he left for Buenos Aires. That was a pretty big statement. That was eight months ago. Are you thinking about trying to salvage your marriage?" Gail was surprised to hear it, especially with a man like Ashley Rowe pursuing her. He had a lot more going for him than her husband did. And he was single and straight and he loved her.

"I don't know what I'm thinking," Oona said. "Maybe Ashley will get tired of me when the novelty wears off. He needs someone his own age. I'm too old and too square for him. I'm not glamorous. One of these days, he'll wake up and see that." It was what she was most afraid of, that he'd decide she wasn't enough for him.

"You bring a lot to the table, Oona. You have a lot to give someone. You need to have more faith in yourself."

"I don't have faith in anyone anymore," Oona said sadly, "least of all in myself and my own judgment. I didn't even realize my husband was gay."

"Neither did he, apparently," Gail said tartly. She wasn't a fan of Charles Webster. He hadn't given Oona a fair shake, and now she had lost faith in herself, even more than in him. "Just given what I know, and what you've told me about Ashley, I think I'd take a chance on him, and get myself to L.A., and give it a shot. You're worried about the age difference. What about the racial issues? Are you worried about that?" Gail asked her squarely.

"Less than everything else. He's an amazing person, but he's younger and famous, and a movie star. What am I doing with a guy like that?"

"Why not?" Gail said confidently. "Why not you? He'd be lucky to be with you. And at least he seems to have the brains to know it. Why not give it a chance? What have you got to lose?"

"A lot, if he dumps me for some thirty-year-old actress, or younger."

"You love him, and his kids. Why not trust that and give it a shot?" Gail made it sound easy, and in Oona's mind it wasn't. To her, it was a trust walk on the high wire without a net under her. "Only you know if you love him enough to take the chance. No one ever knows for sure with any relationship. Some of the best ones don't make it, and the long shots do sometimes. You'll never know unless you try. But I think you'll always regret it if you don't."

"It was easy in France. We were in some kind of bubble. It wasn't real life here. We'll be on real time now if I go to L.A. in the life of a star." Gail hoped for Oona's sake that she'd be brave enough to do it. And Gail suspected that being worried about an interracial relationship might be part of it, even if Oona wasn't aware of it or didn't admit it to herself. It was an added element she'd never had to deal with before, and it was bound to raise additional issues she'd never even thought of. It was one more factor to consider, even if it hadn't been an issue in France. The fact that Ashley was world famous gave them a certain amount of leeway. People would be more likely to accept them because of it in the States. And they couldn't please everyone. Some members of the Black community would criticize him for being with a white woman. Ashley had already said he didn't care.

Ashley was going to be busy filming the series at least for the next two months, so Oona didn't have to make any big decisions immediately, and she had to figure her life out anyway. He was going to be on hiatus for December and part of January, and by then Gail assumed Oona would be back in New York.

Ashley called Oona every day. He didn't pressure her about coming home. He understood that she was hesitant to leave her cozy nest in France. It had shielded her from the world for eight months, and once she was back in New York, she would have to face real life again—her empty apartment, her absent kids, no job to go back to, and the divorce she had decided to file. And he was busy filming the series, and sequestered on the set. If she had been in L.A. then, he wouldn't have been able to see her—he had to begin quarantine for work. Once he started work, the best he could do was call her every day, twice when he had time, and remind her that he loved her. So far, the series was off to a great start and going well. The other actors were major professionals, as he was, some of the biggest in the business, and it was a pleasure working with them. He told Oona how much he was enjoying it, and how much he respected the screenwriter—it was exciting working with the script. But he missed her terribly, and she told him she missed him too. In spite of her worries about the future, her days in France seemed empty once he and the children had left.

After three weeks of aching loneliness after Ashley went to L.A., Oona made the decision that it was time to go back. The figures of new cases in France and patients in the intensive care units in the hospitals were rising sharply, and a second confinement was inevitable. The handwriting was on the wall. It was the second wave scientists had predicted for months, in the States as well, and she decided to leave before it happened. Without Ashley, there was nothing to keep her in France now. He was relieved when she decided to leave France. She would be three thousand miles closer in New York.

She booked a seat on a flight to New York in mid-October, and notified the owners of the house that she would be leaving La Belle Florence, but was sad to leave it nonetheless and hoped she would be back one day. She had tender memories there now, of Ashley and his children, as well as the months she had spent there before they met. It had been a real home for her, and a haven of sorts for eight months, while she healed from her losses. She was deeply grateful to the Hong Kong owners who had allowed her to stay for so long, offering it to her for free for several months of the confinement, and for a very reasonable rent thereafter. It had been a joy to be there, giving her shelter, comfort, and a safe refuge in the storm. She sent them a beautiful silver bowl from Hermès, and bought a cashmere shawl for Marie.

She was sad to leave, and treasured the beautiful miniature Ashley had given her of Florence de Montmarrin with her little dog. She bought a travel bag for her namesake to make the trip.

She warned her housekeeper in New York that she was coming home, let the children know her date of arrival, and sent Charles a brief email. She didn't ask about his plans, since he still seemed to be happy in Buenos Aires and had extended his sabbatical until the end of the year. She wanted to get their situation in order before he returned. He had said that Roberto would have his visa by then, and they would both be going back to the New York office, so they were obviously still together and doing well. And he seemed to expect Oona to remain in the status quo, at least until he got back. He never mentioned a divorce, and she hadn't yet. She wanted to speak to her attorney first. It would be complicated, with the apartment in New York and the house in the Hamptons—they owned both jointly, and she didn't know if he'd agree to sell—but he had said he wouldn't oppose a divorce when he left, if that was what she wanted. She hoped he would be reasonable about it, and assumed he would be since he was still with Roberto. She wasn't looking forward to the legal procedures. It was the end of an era, which had been over for nearly a year. Oona wondered if she would feel freer to move forward with Ashley once she was divorced. In the meantime, she still had moments of anxiety about it, and what the future would look like for them. There was so much they still had to explore, now that he was back at work on a new show. It was expected to be a major hit.

The morning Oona left La Belle Florence, she looked at the gardens for a last time, and at the house that had been her home for eight months. She knew she would never forget it. It was a Sunday, so Marie wasn't there. They had said a tearful goodbye two days before. Oona felt like she was leaving home. And the risk of Covid was high. She put Florence in her travel bag, and had her travel documents with her. She closed the door behind her, and got in the van with all her bags. She had two suitcases filled with the things she had bought at the *brocantes,* and had sent several cartons to New York.

The airport seemed as empty as it had when Ashley left a month before. She checked in and waited outside in the fresh air for as long as she could before her flight.

Ashley knew when she was traveling and was worried about her. She had promised to call as soon as she landed in New York. She had a window seat, which was curtained off, and there was only one other passenger in first class, at the other side of the aircraft. The crew made fewer visits to the passengers than they used to, and the meal was carefully wrapped with all the necessary sanitary precautions. And she kept Florence in her bag for the entire flight. The dog slept most of the way and Oona did the same. She had a lump in her throat when the plane took off and they flew over Paris, and she woke up in time to see Long Island come into view. She had been gone for so long, since she innocently left for France for a month, and it seemed so strange to be coming home. At Ashley's request, the airline sent someone to meet her at the plane, after they landed smoothly and taxied down the runway to the gate.

"Welcome home," she whispered to Florence, and patted her. She went through customs and immigration with ease, and left the airport as quickly as she could. She had hired an SUV to drive her home and filled it with her luggage. It seemed strange to hear people speaking English all around her—she could manage halfway decent French now. She walked the dog as soon as she left the terminal and saw that most people, not all, were wearing masks.

She called Ashley as soon as she got in the car. He was in his trailer studying his lines and waiting for her call, and he answered as soon as he saw her number.

"Are you okay?" he asked her, and she smiled. It was good to hear his deep smooth voice with the accent she loved. It was something familiar to hold on to in what seemed like an unfamiliar world now, and no longer felt like home. "Did everything go okay at the airport?" He'd been worried about her all day. She had gained six hours on the flight—it was only noon in New York, and nine A.M. for him in L.A. She had left Paris in the middle of the night for him, at one-thirty in the morning, and he had lain awake for hours wishing her well, and willing her to be safe.

"It was fine. There was a line at immigration, but the ground agent helped me. And they didn't charge me duty for the things I declared. I said I'd been in France since the pandemic started, and it was too dangerous to come back. By the time I got in the car, I wanted to burn the clothes I'm wearing and take a hot shower when I get home." She didn't have time for the shower, and didn't intend to burn her clothes, just send them to the cleaners.

"That's what we did too, and everyone was fine."

"I'll take a test in a few days, but hopefully I'll be okay." It was something they had to worry about all the time now, which hadn't been true in her rural life in France. She had worried more when they went to Paris, and she and Ashley had gotten tested several times. "How are you?" she asked him. "Everything okay on the set?" There were constant script changes every day, but he was used to it, particularly with a diligent screenwriter. They had hired one of the best in the business, and he had said the script was a pleasure to work with, as were the actors. And she knew they Covid-tested the entire cast and crew every few days to protect them. "It's going to be strange to be home," she said with a sigh. "It was weird to hear people speaking English at the airport." He laughed.

"I felt that way too." He was fluent and Oona's French had improved considerably, she could manage well by then. They talked for a few minutes, and he said he'd call her later when he got off the set. She rode the rest of the way into the city, looking through the window at the outskirts of Manhattan sliding by. It was chilly, but winter hadn't set in yet. She opened the window and felt the air on her face, and half an hour later, they reached her building, and the doorman looked surprised to see her, and helped unload the bags.

"You've been gone a long time," he said, as he loaded the bags into the elevator, and she tipped him generously.

"I've been in France since February," she said.

"Welcome home, Mrs. Webster," he said, which surprised her for an instant, as she had been using "Kelly" since she left, and "Webster" sounded strange to her now. She turned the key in the lock when she got to her apartment, opened the door, pushed her suitcases inside, and stepped in. Bertie, the housekeeper, came from the kitchen to greet her, and burst into tears when she saw her, and she put her mask on as Oona let Florence out of the bag. She had walked her at the airport and stopped for her before they went into the building. Florence ran around the apartment, sniffing everywhere. Bertie looked at her in surprise.

"Who's that?"

"That's Florence." At the sound of her name, she came running back and wagged her tail at Bertie, who bent to pet her.

"I thought you were never coming back," Bertie said, and wiped her eyes. "And Mr. Webster?" she asked, and Oona looked serious for a minute. Bertie knew they'd been separated before Oona left and felt sorry for her.

"He's still in Argentina," Oona said in an even tone.

"Is he coming home soon?"

"I don't know. Traveling is hard to plan these days," Oona said, and walked down the hall to her bedroom with Florence following close behind her, and Bertie helping with the bags. And as Oona walked into her bedroom, it hit her like a tidal wave and took her breath away for a minute. She was home. She had expected everything to be the same, and to feel the same about it. But nothing was the same. Charles was gone, with his new love, and she was alone in the apartment. He had left a month and a half before she did, but she associated him with the apartment, and it was strange not to see him there, and to know he wasn't coming home, not to her anyway. The children's rooms were tidy and unoccupied, and nothing in her life was the same now. Charles was gone, she had no job, and the man she loved was another three thousand miles away. She wanted to try to see Will soon, but nothing had been arranged yet. She took her coat off, intending to send it to the cleaner, and a few minutes later, she went into her bathroom and peeled her clothes off and laid them in a heap to send out too. She didn't want to take any more risks than she had already taken to get home, and as she stood in the shower it became clear to her again that wherever she was, whether in New York or France, her life as she had known it was forever changed, and would never be the same again.

Chapter 12

Oona's first day back in New York, after a fitful sleep and two more calls from Ashley telling her how glad he was that she was back in the States, was a litany of calls she had intended to make for months and was ready to face now. She called Gail to tell her she was home, and they promised each other to have lunch as soon as it seemed reasonable and safe, after Oona had a Covid test, and Gail said she'd have one too.

She had called Will the night before, and texted Meghan to tell her she was home. She called her lawyer and explained the situation to him and told him she wanted a divorce, as clean and as civil as possible. He suggested that it could get complicated over jointly owned property, and suggested that she and Charles discuss it, to see how they wanted to handle it. Oona was planning to go out to East Hampton to see the house there that weekend. It had stood empty for nearly a year, with her handyman checking on it once a week. She hadn't been there since November, and she wanted to see how she felt about it now. She and Charles had too many memories there, happy summers they had spent there with the children when they were small. She wasn't sure she wanted to be there anymore. She was prepared to sell it if Charles was willing, and it should bring a decent amount for each of them. Real estate prices had increased dramatically since they had bought it twenty years before, but had dropped somewhat during the pandemic. When Meghan was two and Will was four, it had been the perfect second home for them then, in East Hampton, which had gained immensely in popularity since. It wasn't a fancy house, but it was a great house for a family with children, and they had maintained it in good condition, and the handyman said it had survived the previous winter without damage or incident. She wanted to see it before she asked Charles to sell it, or offered to sell her half to him. She wanted a last look before she gave it up, to make sure it was what she wanted to do.

She called three headhunters she knew and asked them to put her on their books for an editorial job in publishing. She wasn't expecting to find a job as the head of a house—a senior management position would be satisfactory, or even one as a senior editor where she would work remotely. She didn't have a salary in mind and preferred to leave it open and see what she was offered. All three headhunters she called said much the same thing, that jobs were scarce right now, and that many people in publishing were being laid off. It seemed logical that people would be buying more books in the pandemic, but all of the publishing houses had been shaken by having to close their offices indefinitely, and not knowing how long it would go on, so they were letting people go rather than keep a heavy staff on their payroll. Companies were looking for ways to trim things down and reduce their overhead. And everyone was working remotely, like Gail. Office buildings all over New York were standing empty, unable to be occupied safely, with small offices, shared spaces, and elevators in which only a few people could ride at the same time, due to Covid, with hundreds or even thousands of people in the building needing to use them. No one had been able to figure it out yet, so entire companies were being run from home. Commercial real estate was facing its worst crisis in the history of the city, and none of the health issues had been solved.

The calls weren't encouraging, and she called Gail again after the last one.

"Wow, it's worse than I thought. I called the three best headhunters I know—I used to hire from them—and they all said that no one is hiring right now. They're still laying people off because the pandemic is lasting longer than they expected, and all the big firms are leaving the buildings empty and making no plans to go back until sometime next year."

"That's what I've heard too, but they must need some jobs filled. They can't run their businesses with a skeleton staff, and some people must be getting hired. You'll find something, Oona. It may take some time."

"I wonder if it's like this in every city in the country."

"Any city with buildings like ours will be in the same boat," Gail said matter-of-factly, and Oona wondered if she would find anything at all. They chatted for a few minutes and hung up. Oona looked through the bills that Bertie had been sending her in France.

Oona had forwarded some to Charles in Argentina, like the ones for membership fees at the many clubs he belonged to that were doing him no good now. He had dropped a number of them, keeping others he knew he'd want to use when he got home. Some of them were closed for now, if they were unable to comply with the constantly changing health rules that made using gyms and sports facilities impossible, and their indoor dining rooms were closed too. Gatherings and social events were not allowed. And many of the club members were older and preferred to stay home or at their country properties and estates.

Oona called the bank and transferred some funds. Charles had been wiring her money monthly in France, to help her when she lost her job, but she hadn't spent much while she was there, other than for food and rent, which he hadn't complained about. He was responsible about their money and had always been generous with her. And they had enough savings to be comfortable. He had invested their funds well, although Oona didn't like depending on him, and liked having her own money. She missed her salary, and the severance had run out. Within a few months, she would start to feel the pinch of not having a job to pay for the occasional luxuries she indulged in. She intended to be careful now. She wondered if he was supporting Roberto, although she knew that it was none of her business, but she was curious about their arrangement, and the role Charles played in his life, as responsible husband or generous lover, or if they shared expenses as she and Charles had. They had rarely had disagreements over money, and she wondered if they would now, when they divided things up.

Ashley was still working. Oona sat at her desk and paid bills that night and for a few minutes it felt as though she had never left. It was an odd sensation. When her cell phone rang she expected it to be Ashley, when he finished his scenes for the day, and she was surprised to see Charles's number appear. She picked it up, and for a few seconds there was silence on the line, and then she heard a wrenching sob. She wasn't even sure if it was him, and she was suddenly afraid that Roberto was using Charles's phone and something had happened to Charles. She prayed it wasn't so, and the voice at the other end continued to cry as her heart pounded, and then at last she heard Charles's voice.

"Oh my God, what's wrong . . . Charles, are you all right?" He could barely speak coherently, as she tried to calm him and speak soothingly. And he finally composed himself enough to talk.

"It's Roberto. He caught a cold a few days ago, and he had a terrible sore throat. I was worried it was Covid, and he insisted it wasn't. He said he gets bad colds and always winds up with strep throat. I got him to take a test, and he was positive. That was only two days ago, and he spiked a terrible fever that night. He had a hundred and five temperature when I got him to the hospital the next morning. That was yesterday. He couldn't breathe and they intubated him immediately, and he just got steadily worse. We spent a weekend in Rio de Janeiro ten days ago, and he must have gotten it then. We ate out a lot, and he has a lot of friends there, and no one was wearing masks. They put him in a coma last night in order to administer different meds, but he died two hours ago. Oonie, I can't believe it. He's gone. He was thirty-four years old and he was in perfect health. He'd had asthma as a child, and he must have had weak lungs as a result. His parents live in Uruguay, and they're coming here to get his body and take him home to bury him. They can't even hold a funeral for him. It's not allowed during Covid—only his parents and spouse are allowed at the burial."

"That would be you," she said gently. He was so distraught she was sorry for him. He had truly loved Roberto and was decimated by his death.

"His parents didn't know he was gay. They think I'm just his boss and a friend. I can't tell them now—Roberto wouldn't want that. They're fairly old and they wouldn't understand. It's not fair to upset them more than they are. I can't believe this has happened." He started crying again and it took him several minutes to regain his composure. "I have to quarantine now for a few days, and as soon as I get a negative test, I'm coming home," he said. She hoped he meant New York and not the apartment, but she felt cruel saying it in the condition he was in. "I told his parents I would empty his apartment and send everything to them. They can't come to New York with the borders closed. I can't believe this happened. He was fine five days ago. We played tennis, and the next day he got sick." Oona told him again how sorry she was, and to call her if he needed anything. And since he would be clearing Roberto's apartment in New York, she assumed he would stay there.

She told Ashley about it that night, and called Charles the next day to make sure he was all right. He sounded calmer than he had the day before, but he was in deep grief. Roberto's parents had just taken him a few hours before. And Charles was at serious risk now to catch Covid himself.

"I have to quarantine for five days before I can take a test. I'll fly home as soon as I get the result, if it's negative. I already have a reservation for the flight. I can't stay here now. Roberto's brother is emptying his apartment. I'm staying at a hotel. I had to get all my things out before the family arrived. His brother doesn't know either, but I think he might have guessed. They're all heartbroken over him. He was the youngest child, and apparently a wonderful son. He was such a good person," he said, and Oona felt strange listening to him—it was a clear view of how much Charles had loved Roberto. She felt like a voyeur listening to him, but he needed to talk to someone, and she was the closest person to him after Roberto. She listened to him for half an hour, and he promised to let her know when he got the result of the Covid test. She dreaded the possibility that he had it, and hoped he didn't. It would be too cruel if he got sick now too. She was at her desk, thinking about him, when the phone rang again. It was Will this time.

"You sound very serious," Will said. He sounded like he was in good spirits, and she hated to spoil it, but at least his father was okay for now. And Will had no attachment to Roberto, never having met him. He had refused to, as had Meghan, out of loyalty to their mother, despite their father's offers to introduce them, and assurances that Roberto was a lovely person, and not responsible for the demise of Charles and Oona's marriage, which their children did not believe.

"I was just talking to your father," she said to explain her somber tone.

"Is he okay?" No one was exempt from the risks now, and life could change in an instant, as it just had for Charles and Roberto.

"Yes, he's fine," she confirmed. "But Roberto died yesterday of Covid. Your father is very upset, understandably. Roberto was

young and healthy, and apparently they went to Brazil for a weekend, saw a lot of friends, and they think Roberto got it there."

"And Dad doesn't have it?"

"Not so far. He's in quarantine for five days, and then he'll get a
test. If it's negative, he can fly home. He's terribly shaken by what
happened, and so quickly. From what I can tell, Roberto was only
sick for a few days."

"That does sound awful," Will conceded. "But I have some good
news for you." He paused for a dramatic moment, and Oona hoped
he wasn't calling to tell her he'd gotten engaged. He was much too
young to consider marriage, even with a long engagement. Heather
was more the right age, although she was young too. Will was only
twenty-four, soon to turn twenty-five, but still a long way off from
an ideal time to get married.

"Heather and I got married today," he said in a jubilant tone. He
sounded almost giddy, and for an instant Oona felt like she might
faint, but she didn't.

"Is she pregnant?" Oona blurted out and wished she hadn't. The
words just shot out of her by reflex.

"No, she's not." Will sounded annoyed. "We just didn't want to
wait any longer. We know what we're doing and what we want.
And everything's so crazy with the pandemic. City Hall is closed,
but we got the license online, and Heather has a friend who got
ordained online last year, to marry a friend, so she called him and
he agreed to marry us. We did it in Golden Gate Park, and it was
perfect. It was just what we wanted." He sounded jubilant, and so
young and naïve to Oona. She liked Heather, but Will was too
young to get married, in his mother's opinion.

"Why didn't you wait until your father and I and Meghan could be there?" It seemed to Oona like a brutal rejection of his family.

"Because then Heather's whole huge family would want to come, her parents and grandparents, aunts, uncles, cousins, and all her siblings. And that isn't what we wanted. We wanted to keep it small and private and just the two of us. Aren't you going to congratulate me, Mom?" he asked her, and she had to dredge up from somewhere the semblance of excitement and parental delight, when in fact she was heartbroken that he had done it without her and the rest of their family present, and just the way he had done it proved to her that he was young and impulsive and immature and didn't think things through. She was almost angry, but didn't dare show it.

He passed the phone to Heather, who was euphoric. They acted as though they had invented marriage, and Oona didn't know what more to say to them. She couldn't tell them the truth. She thought Heather had manipulated him into it, but whatever the reason or how they had done it, it felt like a disaster to her, and she was sure the marriage wouldn't last. Heather was a very sweet girl, but she could have waited another five or six years to get married. They were both young enough to have waited. Oona wished they hadn't done it, but it was too late now. The die had been cast, the wedding was unfortunately legal, and all Oona had to do now was pretend to be happy for them. She started to cry as soon as they hung up. She couldn't believe he had done such a stupid thing. He hardly knew Heather, and he had cheated his mother out of being able to attend her only son's wedding. She felt genuine loss over it, and couldn't stop crying.

Ashley called her soon after and could tell she was upset. She was still reeling from the news when Ashley called her. He had called her a few hours before, and nothing was wrong then, but it was now.

"Will just called me," she said in a funereal tone.

"Is he okay?" These days, you never knew—people got sick so quickly, like Roberto.

"He's healthy, if that's what you mean, other than that he is stupid and besotted and immature. He got married in Golden Gate Park today, without his family present, by some friend of Heather's who got ordained online. It wasn't even a proper wedding, just the two of them. He couldn't wait a few weeks until I got out there, if that was what he was going to do?" She was angry and upset and heartbroken all at once, as Ashley tried to console her and calm her down. He knew how much she loved her children, and fully understood how crushed she would be to miss the wedding of either one. It made her feel like a failure as a mother that her son had gone to great lengths to get married without her there to see it, hug him, and wish him well.

"Would you have tried to talk him out of it if you'd been there?" he asked her gently.

"Yes," she said without hesitating.

"That's why he didn't wait. For whatever reason, he wanted to do it now, even without your permission. Is it possible that she's pregnant?"

"That was the first thing I asked him, and he said no," she said, and blew her nose. Nothing had been easy since she'd gotten back to New York. There were no jobs, Roberto had died so Charles was upset and returning, and now Will had married so absurdly young and who knew if Heather was the right girl and whether the marriage would last. And Oona was missing Ashley. He was the one calm, constant, stable force in her life. She'd had so many doubts about him because he was a star, but she always seemed to be able to rely on him to be there for her and say the right thing. He was mature beyond his years, and eight years between them was beginning to seem like not such an insurmountable obstacle after all. He was a responsible adult.

"I know it's hard, but I think you have to be supportive of him now. He's not going to get it annulled. He did it, and you don't want to damage the relationship you have with him. Particularly if it doesn't work out. Then he'll need you more than ever, and if you alienate him now, he won't want to come to you afterward. It will mean you were right, which will be hard for him for a long time. As painful as it is for you, you need to embrace it, for as long as it lasts. And if it doesn't, then to help him pick up the pieces when it falls apart."

"She's a perfectly nice girl," Oona conceded, "and we had a nice time with her when she came to France with him before the pandemic started, but who knows if she's the right one for the rest of his life. That is such a huge decision and it's so easy to get it wrong." She certainly had, she knew now.

"Maybe they'll get it right," he said, trying to cheer her, although he agreed with her, having married too young himself and made a mistake. "And if they don't make it, you'll be there, and he'll learn a big lesson and do better next time. He'll be more mature then. And maybe she's good for him now."

"I hope so," she said wanly, feeling overwhelmed by circum-stances. Everything was so difficult. She wanted Meghan to come home from Africa before January, and she wouldn't do that either, and clearly, Will had lost his mind.

Oona was still vastly upset when Charles called her a week later. Will had told her he called his father too, but Charles was too upset about Roberto to discuss Will's marriage with him. And he didn't want to talk to Oona about it either.

Charles called her again the following week. "How are you?" she asked him sympathetically. He sounded better, but still very sad, understandably. And at least he hadn't caught Covid from Roberto.

"About the same. I still can't believe it happened. I just wanted to let you know that I got a negative test again," he confirmed. "I don't have Covid, remarkably, as we were together all the time. I'm flying home tomorrow. I'll be landing late. I didn't want to scare you and make you think I was a burglar. I'll just let myself in. Don't wait up for me." Oona felt like she'd been shot when she heard what he said.

"Why would I think I'm being burglarized?" she said, hoping she had misunderstood him. He couldn't have meant what he said.

"I thought that if you hear someone walk in, in the middle of the night, it might frighten you," he explained.

"You're not planning to stay here, are you?" she asked, shocked.

"Well, yes, I don't want to stay at Roberto's. I'll pack it up for his parents, but I don't want to stay there. I thought I'd stay at the apartment. Technically, I still live there and we're still married."

"You've been living with someone else for eleven months. You can't just waltz back in here now because he's dead. I'm sorry to be so blunt, but you could have asked me." She hadn't intended to tell him over the phone, but she had no choice. "I called a lawyer when I got home. I want a divorce, Charles," she said quietly.

"Now? With Roberto gone? I want to stay home for a while before we do anything radical. You've waited this long. And Roberto's death changes everything." She couldn't believe what she was hearing. And once again, it was all about him, just as it had been when he left her to stay with Roberto before they went to Buenos Aires together.

"No, it doesn't 'change everything.' I'm sure it does for you, but it doesn't for me. You left for some very strong reasons after falling in love with someone else, who just happened to be a man. But man or woman, you left me. It's taken me a year to adjust to it. Now you can't just conveniently move back in because your boyfriend died. I'm very sorry that he did, but you killed our marriage for me. You shattered my faith in the human race for a while, and in myself. You can't come back here. There is nothing for you to come home to. Our marriage is over—you don't live here anymore."

"If nothing else, we own the apartment jointly. We can discuss the rest when I get home." He sounded cold, and she was angry at how presumptuous he was, and entitled.

"There is nothing to discuss. Our marriage is over for me. You killed it, and I don't want to bring it back from the dead. I understand that you need to mourn, and I'm sorry this is terrible for you. But you can't stay in this apartment as long as I'm living here."

"Oona, I want to come back to you. I love you—I always have. I need to get over Roberto, but I think we can work out our differences and make this work again." She couldn't believe what she was hearing.

"There's nothing to work out. You're gay, and I'm not."

"My relationship with Roberto was an aberration. It won't happen again. You and I lived together before."

"Supposedly, you didn't know you were gay then, and neither did I. Now we do. And you have to live with the choices you made, even though Roberto isn't coming home with you. You'll have to stay somewhere else." He had never heard her sound that way before. It was obvious that she meant it, and he was shocked. How could she not let him stay at the apartment, after what he had just been through? It didn't make sense to him, but it did to her. He didn't want to stay at a hotel, and the rest of his things were still at the apartment.

He wrote her a text, asking her to reconsider before he flew home the next day, and she responded with the single word "No" and then turned off her phone.

She was still fuming when she went to bed that night, thinking of his absolute and complete selfishness, wanting to stay with her and even talk about their getting their marriage fixed, and living a lie again. It was beyond belief, and on the heels of Will telling her that he had gotten married in such a stupid way. She finally fell asleep, just before morning came, exhausted by two of the three men in her life. At least Ashley was a reasonable person and he loved her, and she loved him.

Chapter 13

Charles arrived in New York the following day and stayed at The Mark, a few blocks from the apartment. He called Oona the next morning and asked to come to see her, and she agreed to meet with him. She wasn't trying to avoid him, but she wasn't looking forward to it. The conversation they needed to have was long overdue. It didn't matter what happened with Ashley. Whatever they did, her marriage to Charles was over and it needed to be buried.

He came on time, rang the bell politely, and she let him in. Bertie had left for the day, which Oona had arranged on purpose. She didn't want her celebrating his homecoming like the conquering hero. He didn't live there anymore, unless he wanted to buy her half of the apartment from her. She thought they should put it on the market. She didn't want to buy it from him. She thought they both needed a fresh start, and she knew she did. Seeing him again was odd, he felt like a stranger to her. It felt like their marriage was years behind them, not just months. He looked thinner and older, and his eyes were sad after Roberto.

She offered him a cup of coffee, which he declined. She didn't offer him wine because she didn't want him to get maudlin about their marriage. She wanted to keep it as dry and businesslike as possible. He spent the first half hour talking about Roberto's final moments, which seemed inappropriate to her, and then she reiterated to him that she was filing for divorce, and they had decisions to make about the apartment and the house in East Hampton.

"I want another chance," he said to her in a pleading tone. "After twenty-five years, we deserve that."

"You forgot that a year ago. You can't take back the last year. If Roberto hadn't died, would you be asking to come back now? That's opportunistic, and just plain wrong."

"Is there someone else?" he asked her. She had never told him about Ashley. It was none of his business. He had Roberto, and she had a right to someone too, and she didn't want to have to explain to him who Ashley was, that he was a film star, eight years younger, and of another race. He had no right to that information. She owed him nothing now.

"That's irrelevant," she said coldly.

"No, it's not," he said firmly. "Is that why you stayed in France for so long?"

"No, it isn't. I was safer there. Neither you nor the kids were home, so I stayed. I had nothing to come home to," thanks to him, but she didn't say it.

"I don't want a divorce," he said.

"I don't need your permission, I can file it without your consent, and divorce you without it. It would be better for both of us if we can make the financial decisions amicably. But if we can't I'm still filing for divorce. You can buy my half of the apartment if you want it, or we can sell it. I'm going out to East Hampton this weekend, to look at the house and see how I feel about it. I'm not sure about that yet. I might want to stay there this winter if the pandemic continues, but honestly, I think it will be too depressing. The weather is so grim there in the winter."

"I wanted to spend time there with Roberto," he said wistfully.

"I'm sorry," she said softly. She could see how much pain he was in, and yet he wanted to be married to her again, because it was an easy solution for him, if she was willing—but she wasn't.

Charles left the apartment a little while later, lost in his own thoughts as he walked back to The Mark. He was thinking about everything Oona had said. He wanted to convince her to try again. With Roberto gone, he didn't want a new life—he wanted the old one, like an old pair of slippers that fit comfortably with no effort. But it would never be that way again. Too much had happened, and Roberto would always be between them. And her feelings for Charles were dead, except as ancient history.

And Ashley was an important part of the equation for her. More and more she'd been thinking of the things he had said to her. He called her faithfully morning and night. She had called Simon and Alana to make sure they were all right and weren't too lonely without their father. Ashley had been touched when Simon told him about it. He reported to his father that Oona didn't know when she was coming to L.A., but she loved them.

She went out to East Hampton on Saturday. There was a dusting of snow on the ground, and the house was cold, dark, and empty when she walked in. Her mind flooded with the memories of the happy times there, and there had been so many. If she was living a lie then, at least she didn't know it, and now it didn't matter. The people they had been then were gone forever. Charles had changed course radically, and was lost, trying to find his way back. And she had become her own person. She could no longer follow him blindly. Ashley just wanted her to be happy, and to love and protect her. He didn't have Charles's demons, or anything to gain from her joining him in his fortunate life. He just wanted to share it with her, and even if there were hard moments later, he wanted to be there with her and to work them out with her. Charles wanted to re-create the past, and use her as balm for his loss of the man he truly loved. Ashley was offering her a clean future, with their past mistakes behind them. She and Ashley would make new ones, but it was a fresh start, in a very different world.

She closed the door to the house in East Hampton and had the answer she'd wanted. She couldn't go back. If Charles wanted it, he could have it. It wasn't her house anymore. She wasn't the same person. And the memories would go with her.

* * *

She was planning to have lunch with Gail that week. Gail was having a Covid test on Monday, and Oona was too. They would get their results on Tuesday or Wednesday, and then they could have lunch together.

Gail called her on Tuesday afternoon, sounding depressed.

"I can't believe it. I hardly go anywhere. I wear a mask whenever I go out. But I tested positive, so I can't have lunch with you. I have to be in quarantine for ten days. We can have lunch after that. I'm sorry, Oona."

"Me too. But don't be silly. We'll have lunch when you're okay. Do you feel sick?" Oona was worried about her friend.

"I'm asymptomatic for now. That's something at least. But I wanted to see you."

"Me too. We will." Oona started going through old files and letters that night. She had them spread all over her desk when she got a call from an unfamiliar number, and a woman's voice spoke to her when she answered. It was Heather, her daughter-in-law, and she tried to shift gears to be nice to her and not angry about the wedding. Ashley was right. She had to make her peace with it, or she'd lose Will.

"Hi, Heather, how are you?" Oona asked pleasantly.

"Not so good," Heather said, sounding young and scared. "I just dropped Will off at the hospital, and I wanted to tell you. He tested positive two days ago, and now he's got a cough and a fever." Oona felt a chill run down her spine when she told her. "They wouldn't let me stay with him at the hospital. I had a test too and I'm negative. He doesn't know how he got it. He had a haircut last week and he had his mask off, so he thinks he might have gotten it at the barber. Or maybe from an Uber."

"Does he have his phone with him?"

"Yes, but he was feeling pretty rotten from the fever. All they gave him was Tylenol. He might be asleep." She sounded like a child while she told Oona what room he was in, and everything the doctor had said. His oxygen level was low, so they had admitted him instead of sending him home. They wanted to keep an eye on him. "There's no point coming out. They won't let you see him. I can't see him either, unless he gets worse. Then he can only have one person." And that would be Heather, his wife. Oona knew she couldn't fight it. Ashley was right.

Oona called Charles and told him, and he thanked her. Heather had already texted Meghan. She was good about giving all of them daily reports. For two days Will stayed the same, and then he got markedly worse and they admitted him to the ICU. Oona was terrified they would put him on a respirator, in an induced coma, but he was still breathing on his own. When they put him in the ICU, Oona packed a bag that night. He couldn't talk on the phone because it took too much air to do so. He was hooked up to an oxygen machine, and they allowed Heather to see him once for a few minutes, which wasn't a good sign. It meant he was seriously at risk.

She called the airline after Heather's last report, caught a seven A.M. flight to San Francisco, and landed at ten A.M. local time. She had Florence with her and went straight to Will and Heather's apartment when she got there, to drop off the dog. Heather had said she could. Heather answered the door in a bathrobe and looked like she'd been crying. She went straight into Oona's arms, and they hugged each other and sat by the phone for the rest of the day, waiting for news. And Florence sat at Oona's feet, as though she knew something bad had happened.

Oona didn't want him to end up like Ashley's ex-wife or Roberto. They were both young, and Claire had health issues, but according to Charles, Roberto didn't, other than asthma as a child. It was a vicious virus that stole some and spared others and there was no telling who it would be. Will was in the ICU for a week, and Oona and Heather kept each other company for seven agonizing days of waiting for the latest reports from the Covid team at the hospital. They were good about calling and sharing his current status. Three days after Oona had flown, she had a PCR test to make sure she hadn't caught Covid on the trip. It wasn't required, but it was the responsible thing to do. There was no quarantine on entering California. The test was negative.

Will still couldn't talk on the phone, but he was fever-free after a week, though he had lost his sense of taste and smell, and finally, two days later, he was allowed to call them. He sounded tired, and he was hoarse, but he was no longer in danger.

Ashley knew Oona was in San Francisco and called her frequently for updates too. They had been the longest days of Oona's life, and Meghan called whenever she could. She was terrified she would lose her brother. It had reminded all of them that no matter how young and healthy, they were all at risk of catching the virus, and no matter how careful you were, there was a constant margin of error and unpredictability. It struck where it chose and was merciless.

Oona had found a small hotel in Pacific Heights that was open and allowed dogs, and she stayed there. Will and Heather didn't have a guest room. But she and Heather had had plenty of time to talk since Oona had gotten there. The two women had found a comfortable level of entente that centered entirely around Will. And Oona could tell that Heather loved him.

Will was weak and exhausted when he got home, and had never been as tired in his life, but he was alive and on the road to recovery. He was no longer contagious. The doctors believed he would make a full recovery soon. When Oona first saw him, she had tears in her eyes. He looked like he had lost ten or fifteen pounds and his eyes were sunken, but they were bright and lively, and he hadn't lost his sense of humor. He looked thrilled to see his wife and mother.

In the end, it had been nearly three weeks of anxious days and terrifying nights, but he was no longer in danger. Even he couldn't believe all that he'd been through. When he'd been home for a few days, and was anxious to get out, Oona had breakfast with him and then they went for a walk. The world had never looked as bright and shining to Will. He was still exhausted and tired easily.

"Thank you for being here with Heather, Mom, while I was in the hospital. She said you were really nice to her. I know you're mad about our getting married, and how we did it. Thank you for not taking it out on her."

"We were both worried about you," she said as they walked slowly. He still got short of breath easily. "Nothing else mattered. The pandemic has been the great equalizer. No one is exempt, and who lives and who dies is unpredictable. We just didn't want it to be you. She's a good girl and she loves you, no matter how you got married. You have a right to make your own decisions." He had survived his trial by fire and had won her respect. And Oona had learned some things about herself while praying he'd recover. One had to seize the good moments, because life could change in an instant. She wondered now if Charles had been right, to abandon everything for the man he loved. It had ended all too quickly for Roberto, and for Charles as a result. They had spoken every day while Will was sick. He was still in deep mourning for Roberto and had agreed to whatever Oona wanted. The house, the apartment, their material possessions, even his job no longer mattered to him. He didn't care about becoming CEO. He realized that he had wasted years waiting, instead of living. His life had been empty until he met Roberto, and he and Oona had lost each other along the way. Neither of them could figure out when. And he no longer cared what anyone thought of his being gay.

In the same vein, Will knew he'd been right to marry Heather. It had been a decision, not an accident, even if his mother didn't approve. He was man enough now to live with the fallout of his mother's anger, rather than miss the opportunity. And Oona knew now that he had done the right thing, and she thought the marriage would endure. Heather had been strong and caring and compassionate, while they waited hour by hour and day by day, and she had won her mother-in-law's respect.

The same was true of Meghan. Oona didn't like the career path she was choosing, but it was her passion, and she had to live it fully, or feel cheated and useless forever. It made the loss of Oona's career seem insignificant. She liked the security the job gave her, and the money. It was satisfying but not her passion. And no one was better because of it, except a handful of young intellectuals writing for a tiny audience of literary snobs. The world wasn't a better place because of her imprint, and now that mattered to her.

While Will had been sick, he had decided to go to graduate school for a combined business and law degree, and Heather supported it. She had a good job and Will had some money saved. They would manage, and Oona would help if she could, and Charles said he would too. Will didn't want to end up like his father, in a meaningless job thirty years later and a life that had become a lie years earlier than he admitted. Roberto had helped Charles face the truth and become the man he had never been before they met. Whom he loved had allowed him to become real, whatever others thought. He no longer cared. It was the legacy Roberto had left him: himself. Had Roberto lived, Charles suspected now that they would have stayed in Buenos Aires. Without him, he had come home to be more than he'd been before.

Charles quit his job while Will was sick. He wanted to spend the final chapters of his career working for a foundation with global impact, not in advertising in a job that didn't challenge him, waiting to become CEO, which would mean even less now, and feed his ego more than his brain.

Oona knew she had her own decisions to make about Ashley, not about his age or her own, or the starlets who might catch his eye in future, or whether or not she was equal to joining him on the red carpet. It was about whether or not she had the courage to have a full life with him, and stand beside him whatever people thought, no matter what color he was, or how old or young he was, and whether his new series was a failure or a success. They loved each other and she was proud to be with him. That was all that mattered in the end. She'd been hiding not from him, but from herself. She'd done a great deal of soul-searching while Will was sick, and she couldn't let her own fears and other people's opinions make her choices for her. He'd been honest and faithful to her since the day they met. He was due for a week off the set, the week after Will came home and they knew he'd recover. It was her turn now, if she was brave enough to step forward, and follow her heart.

She had dinner with Will and Heather the night before she left. Will was looking better day by day and had gained back a little weight. Heather was busy cooking for him, and the three of them laughed and had a good time. It had been a long time since Oona had laughed and enjoyed her life fully. She realized that now. She and Charles had stopped having fun together years before. They had filled the void between them with their children and their jobs. She had no excuses now if she wanted a life with Ashley. No one was standing in her way, except herself.

She had a return ticket to New York, and she changed it at the airport the next day. She had the small rolling carry-on bag she had brought with her when she had packed in half an hour to come to San Francisco, after Heather called her, and she had Florence in her travel bag. She had nothing glamorous to wear when she saw him, just jeans and sweaters and T-shirts and the running shoes she was wearing. She could shop in L.A. She had had another Covid test the day before, to be responsible.

Oona knew what Ashley was doing that day, and what time he

was leaving the set to go home. The kids were eager to see him after two weeks, and he'd have a week with them now, spend three days isolated afterward, and have a test before he went back to the set. They were rigorous about their protocols, and there hadn't been a single case of Covid on the set so far. The cast and crew were all getting a week off for Thanksgiving, and wrapping the first season in December. If they got green-lighted for a second season, they'd come back in January. They were almost sure of a second season now, and Ashley loved the show. He thought it was the best work he'd ever done, and the audiences would love it. There was something in it for everyone—pathos, drama, love, danger, heartbreak, and hope.

Oona took a cab from the airport in L.A. an hour before Ashley was due to leave the set. She walked to the main gate and told the guards she was meeting Ashley Rowe, and by some miracle, they let her in without a pass. She didn't look dangerous or like a crazed fan. She looked like a serious woman, and they took a chance. She was walking down the main road of the studio as Ashley drove out five minutes later. Her timing was perfect. He saw Oona walking toward him, with her long red hair in a loose bun, with wisps blown around her face in the wind. She wasn't wearing makeup— she'd had a rugged few weeks. It was noon, and he had been shooting since six o'clock that morning and looked impeccable as usual, in a brown leather jacket, a beige turtleneck sweater, jeans, and brown suede boots, with his hair in the distinctive style he never changed whatever the role. He hadn't seen her since he left France six weeks before, but they had talked every day, sometimes several times. He stopped the car and got out, and she smiled at him and didn't say a word as he walked toward her.

"Need a ride?" he asked her, as a slow smile came over his face, and she nodded. "Where are you going?" he asked her.

"Home," she said, "with you, if you'll have me." Their whole future together was in the first word.

Chapter 14

Ashley and Oona spent Thanksgiving with Simon and Alana. Oona had cooked her annual meal. She had bought a tablecloth for his table, which he didn't have, with embroidered napkins. She had set a pretty table and made a perfect meal. Will and Heather were in Salt Lake City with her family, and Meghan had helped cook the meal for her coworkers at the camp. She was going back to the States in a month, and hoped to come back to Kenya in February if they reassigned her, but she would have two months at home first, in San Francisco with her brother, with her mother in L.A., and in New York to see her father and her friends.

Charles was spending Thanksgiving with friends. He and Oona had come to an agreement. He was buying the house in East Hampton from her, and was planning to live there for the remainder of the pandemic. He would decide where he wanted to be after that. But East Hampton was a safe refuge for him now. They were selling the apartment in the city. The rest was easier to sort out after that. Their divorce would be final in a little less than a year, since they had come to an agreement amicably. And when it was final, they would both be free. They already were. He had freed them both when he left for Buenos Aires, although it didn't seem that way then.

Thanksgiving was very different for Oona than it had been the year before. There was no tension in the air, no shattering announcement three days later. Oona mentioned Claire when she said grace. She and Ashley and the children played games afterward, and watched a movie. It was the happiest Thanksgiving she'd had since her own children were small. And both of them called her. Will was feeling well again, and Meghan was excited about coming home. Oona couldn't wait to see her. She was coming to L.A. to visit after she saw her brother and Heather.

It was a perfect day, and Ash's series had just been green-lighted for a second season. They had much to be thankful for. Ashley and Oona had been spotted having dinner together at a restaurant a few days before, and a photo appeared in the tabloids. They weren't a secret anymore. They were ready. Ashley waved at the paparazzi as they left the restaurant, and told her to smile, and he put an arm around her. She did as he told her, and the picture was cute when it showed up in the tabloids. Alana cut it out and put it on her bulletin board. Simon high-fived them when he saw it, and Oona and Ashley laughed.

For Christmas, Ashley had a surprise for them all. He had chartered a huge boat for two weeks, to float around the Caribbean.

They met the yacht in Antigua, and he'd chartered a plane to get them there safely from L.A. He was on hiatus until February. It was a spectacular yacht, and they would be stopping in Tobago. Simon and Alana were excited to see their cousins, and were exploring the boat and making friends with the crew, when a van pulled up on the dock and three people emerged. Ashley smiled broadly when he saw them and waved, just as Oona came back on deck after checking out their cabin.

The three people from the van were wearing masks as they came up the passerelle and Oona stared at them, and then at Ashley.

"Oh my God. . . ." she said as she watched them, and there were tears in her eyes when she was sure. It was Heather, Will, and Meghan. They were his surprise for Oona. There were screams and hugs and laughter as they all hugged, and he hugged them too, and Alana and Simon joined them, and Florence barked and ran around them on the deck.

"How did you do that?" she asked Ashley, breathless. The plan to surprise her had gone seamlessly. They had all cooperated, and no one had slipped in the weeks before.

"You're not the only efficient one around here," he said, and kissed her.

They were standing on deck together as the boat motored out of the port a few minutes later. They'd been waiting for the new arrivals and Oona hadn't known it. She'd thought they were just getting organized at the dock. They were ready for their big adventure. They were his Christmas gift to her.

Ashley and Oona stood on deck watching the port shrink away,

his arm around her, as they headed out to sea, on their way to Tobago. It was a new life in a brave world. She had a whole new
family to meet, and all their children on board with them. The
pieces of their life fit together perfectly.

Ashley held her tightly next to him and smiled down at her. "I've
been working on our summer plans," he said, as the warm wind
brushed their faces, and she looked up at him.

"Isn't it a little early to do that now?" She had only recently
begun to realize how organized he was and how efficient at making plans, as he had just done, getting her children to the boat to
surprise her. She loved that about him—they were partners and
equals, each with their strengths and talents that complemented
each other.

"I've rented a house in France for us, for next summer. I think
you'll like it. Great location—it has a pool, lovely gardens, and
comes with a housekeeper," he said.

"In the south of France?"

"No, actually, in the Essonne region, an hour or so from Paris."
He couldn't repress a smile as he said it, and she looked stunned
as she guessed.

"La Belle Florence?" He broke into a broad smile when he answered.

"I think that she would want us to have it. And your landlords
have been very amenable. I rented it from June until the end of
December next year, for my summer hiatus. Covid should be history by then, so we can go whenever we have a break. I think Florence de Montmarrin would be pleased." Oona put her arms around
him and kissed him. She was beaming. There were only good sur-

prises with Ashley. And he added yet another one. "There's an option to buy in our lease. And I think I can convince them, if you want to buy it." He had just been handsomely paid for the second season, and the Hong Kong owners were interested in the deal. Ashley was fairly sure he could close it if Oona wanted the house as much as he did. It had deep sentimental significance for them. "I think Florence would approve." He held Oona in his arms and smiled at her. "I'm a lucky man," he said, and kissed her. "You've changed my life, Oona," he said softly. And he had changed hers. Life with him was full of blessings and surprises, acts of kindness, and tender moments. He wanted to give her the house as a wedding present when her divorce came through, but that was a surprise for another day, maybe next Christmas. In the meantime he wanted to show her the Tobago of his childhood, share his family with her, and enjoy their children on the boat and at La Belle Florence next summer. They had so much to look forward to.

About the Author

DANIELLE STEEL has been hailed as one of the world's best-selling authors, with a billion copies of her novels sold. Her many international bestsellers include *Trial by Fire, Triangle, The Ball of Versailles, Joy, Resurrection, Only the Brave, Never Too Late, Upside Down,* and other highly acclaimed novels. She is also the author of *His Bright Light,* the story of her son Nick Traina's life and death; *A Gift of Hope,* a memoir of her work with the homeless; *Expect a Miracle,* a book of her favorite quotations for inspiration and comfort; *Pure Joy,* about the dogs she and her family have loved; and the children's books *Pretty Minnie in Paris* and *Pretty Minnie in Hollywood.*

daniellesteel.com
Facebook.com/DanielleSteelOfficial
Twitter: @daniellesteel
Instagram: @officialdaniellesteel

About the Type

This book was set in Charter, a typeface designed in 1987 by Matthew Carter (b. 1937) for Bitstream, Inc., a digital typefoundry that he cofounded in 1981. One of the most influential typographers of our time, Carter designed this versatile font to feature a compact width, squared serifs, and open letterforms. These features give the typeface a fresh, highly legible, and unencumbered appearance.